Night Hawk

Other Five Star Titles
by Stephen Overholser:

Dark Embers at Dawn
Cold Wind
Double-Cross
Shadow Valley Rising
Fire in the Rainbow
West of the Moon
Chasing Destiny

NIGHT HAWK

A Western Story

Stephen
Overholser

Five Star • Waterville, Maine

First Edition, Second Printing.

Published in 2006 in conjunction with
Golden West Literary Agency

Set in 11 pt. Plantin by Elena Picard.

Printed in the United States on permanent paper.

Library of Congress Cataloging-in-Publication Data

Overholser, Stephen.
   Night hawk : a western story / by Stephen Overholser.
  —1st ed.
      p. cm.
   ISBN 1-59414-338-2 (hc : alk. paper)
   1. Ranch life—Fiction. I. Title.
PS3565.V43N54 2006
  813'.54—dc22   2005028615

Night Hawk

Chapter One

Everything west of the Missouri went to hell by wire, barbed or telegraph, after pastures were fenced and poles erected across the wide prairie. When steel rails were laid, the floodgates opened.

All manner of folks journeyed West—swift and slow, young and old, town and country, straight and crooked. Whether escaping the past or embracing the future, all of them were determined to make a life for themselves on the frontier. A generation of settlers sprung from this pioneer seed, as the historians write in their tomes. Diarists of the era remind us their very survival often depended on luck, a twist of fate, nothing more.

In those days the greenest greenhorn on a cattle ranch was usually a fresh-faced kid who had drifted West, a "maverick" cut loose from kin for one reason or another. On the Circle L Ranch that autumn the ramrod hired such a kid to work as wrangler by day and night hawk after sundown.

That scrawny kid booted off the train in Coalton was not so much lean and mean as he was just plain skin and bones. As the old saw has it, he was so skinny that he had to stand up twice to cast a shadow. Over an angular jaw, his cheek bones poked out to twin points in a narrow, sun-bronzed face. His shoulders were bony, and he could just about hang his hat on his hip. The kid was wound as tightly as a watch spring, and anyone who rode with him in those days will not soon forget his gray, coyote eyes peering into to-morrow, or trying to.

Outside of Coalton, the kid was caught riding in a freight car and booted off the train. First, he hid. At dusk he emerged from a tangle of brush down by the creek and drifted, coyote-like, from one end of town to the other as he made his way past the depot to the back stoop of Bertha's Home Cooking Café.

Eyes downcast, he begged for food from residents and cadged coins from train passengers. Pickings were slim. Twice weekly a scattering of passengers waited while the eastbound switched at Coalton to the spur leading to the Black Diamond, an anthracite mine five miles south of town. Coal was loaded into cars out there where Italian miners bunked year around. Closer to town, livestock was shipped by local ranchers at the Coalton siding. From there, Union Pacific cars rolled across the prairie all the way to Chicago.

Trails crossed when Tyler Johnson, ramrod of the Circle L, drove the buckboard on a supply run from the ranch to Coalton. He left the wagon at the mercantile with his list, and walked to the Union Pacific office in the depot. After reserving fifteen cattle cars for the third week of October, he was hailed by Sheriff Wade Rogers.

"You're just the man I'm looking for, Ty."

Shaking hands, the two men angled across Front Street to the saloon district. There, over two-cent cigars and nickel mugs of beer in the Comet Saloon, Rogers mentioned the shadowy presence of the kid.

Ty listened as the sheriff spoke in earnest. Rotund and

8

full-bearded, Rogers was a stout dandy in his navy suit and black vest, a gent sporting the narrow-brimmed hat of a city man. Over the years Ty had encountered numerous lawmen, and, all appearances aside, this one had earned his respect as a fair-minded upholder of the law.

Ty could use a youngster willing to work, one who would keep up with the chores around the place, but the Circle L was too far away for him to hire a town kid. As for ranch hands—with the exceptions of castrating, de-horning, and branding—few would lower themselves to any task out of reach from the saddle or the end of a rope, and certainly no chore that involved the business end of a shovel, hoe, axe, or saw. That left the ramrod and Cornelius, the cook, to pick up the slack.

"Kid claims he's eighteen," Rogers said now. "Fourteen, maybe fifteen, is more like it."

He went on to say the night deputy had caught him in the act of using a Green River knife to jimmy the lock in the back door of Bertha's café. Summoned to the jailhouse, Rogers confronted the kid. He threatened him with lengthy confinement until he figured out that was what he wanted all along—food and a roof. Rogers turned him out in the night with a vague threat of imposing a sentence of hard labor on a diet of bread and water. He advised him to hop the next train out of Coalton.

The kid did as he was told, but was caught even before the engine had built a head of steam. Cornered by railroad bulls in a boxcar, he flashed his knife. The U.P. men closed in. One swung a brakeman's bar. It struck the kid's bony forearm, knocking the knife from his grasp to skitter across floorboards out of the car. The other men laid into him, wielding saps.

Beaten and booted again, the kid recovered his knife in

the weeds and crawled through willows to the muddy bank
of the creek. For the rest of the day and all night he laid on
cool, damp earth, knees drawn up. After dawn he was able
to breathe without crying out in pain. Starting that night, he
took to stealing eggs out of chicken coops and rifling garbage pails for rotting vegetables and anything else that was
remotely edible.

Located in northern Colorado, Coalton was a small town
on a big prairie. Residents soon figured out their nocturnal
bandit was not a raccoon. The collective voices of taxpayers
swelled in a crescendo demanding the sheriff perform his
lawful duty: *Arrest that footloose boy.* Aside from outright
thievery, a feral kid sneaking around at all hours was a bad
influence on town boys.

In Rogers's line of work, simple requests from the citi-
zenry were easier said than done. *So a circuit judge convicts
him of vagrancy. So we put him in jail. So then what?* Most
folks had not thought the issue through to its logical end,
namely the kid's becoming a ward of the town until something else could be done with him.

In larger towns across the West, it was not uncommon
for runaway youths to turn up in railroad depots. Famished
and bedraggled, most sought shelter from the elements and
begged for kitchen hand-outs. An unspoken policy in some
burgs was to pass the hat, collect enough money for a box
lunch and a ticket to the next town down the line, and quietly pass the problem on.

Sheriff Rogers favored that solution, and spoke before
the town council about it. "Money well spent in the long
run," he argued, and was promptly voted down.

One other factor swayed his thinking on this matter.
Morning air carried a crisp hint of the coming change of
seasons. Sheriff Rogers knew winter sometimes hammered

these prairie lands early, and the prospect of discovering the frozen corpse of a youth clad in rags was daunting even to a seasoned lawman.

Still, no one in Coalton offered to contribute to the well-being of a thieving beggar, youthful or not. If the town council weakened, ran the prevailing opinion, word would spread with vagrants far and wide stampeding to Coalton for "free money".

Sheriff Rogers lowered his beer mug and glanced around. The plank floor of the Comet was sprinkled with sawdust, the walls decorated with glass-eyed heads of buffalo, deer, elk, pronghorn above wainscoting. At the foot rail, spittoons were spaced six feet apart. A fleur-de-lis pattern in the pressed tin ceiling added a decorative touch.

The ramrod and the lawman leaned against the long bar with a few other midday patrons. At either end, pickles and hard-boiled eggs filled clear glass demijohns like specimens preserved in formaldehyde. On the other side of the bar, an elaborately carved backbar framed a large mirror, the reflection doubling images of long-necked liquor bottles.

This view gave the barkeep, Ray Owens, a panorama of the saloon's interior when his back was turned. Trouble spotted early usually gave him enough time to enforce a Western tradition: a man had to be able to stand to be deemed fit for another drink. If Ray saw a patron draped over the bar with a boot braced against the foot rail, that gent, even a regular, was invited to leave.

Setting the mug down on the bar now, Rogers eyed a residue of beer foam as though reading tea leaves. The kid was on his mind. Across the Colorado border, Laramie, Wyoming was the nearest main line from the Coalton spur. If no one came forward to do the right thing, Rogers would buy a one-way ticket to Laramie himself and send the kid on his way before winter set in. The favored option, though, was for Ty to take a flyer on this kid. That would solve a lawman's dilemma and at once fill a job opening on the ranch.

"I don't believe the kid's mean," Sheriff Rogers went on. "Way I see it, he's more scared than anything else."

"Scared. Of what?"

"Not knowing where his next meal is coming from," Rogers answered. "Or who will hand him another beating. Railroad bulls did a proper job on him when he followed my advice and hopped a U.P. freight that had stopped to take on water."

Ty thought about that. "You're asking me to hire a kid who's a thief and a liar . . . and not very good at either profession."

The lawman grinned and nodded. "That's about how it stacks up, Ty."

"What name does this kid go by?"

Rogers shrugged. "Smith or Jones. He's claimed three or four names since he landed here."

"What else does he claim?"

"Says he knows horses."

"He does, huh?"

"I already asked Jim down at the livery," the lawman went on. "He's not looking to hire anybody right now."

Skeptical as he was about taking on a kid who was probably a runaway with good reason to run, Ty had hired riders over the years without ever questioning a man's word or investigating his back trail. He decided to give this kid the same benefit of the doubt.

Their first meeting was convened over root beer at the bar of the Comet. Ty watched the kid slug down the sweet drink, and ordered another for him. With Rogers looking on, Ty sized up the shaggy-haired kid as though eyeing a colt sprung from a box cañon.

This one looked as wild as any broomtail. Even with a full head of tangled hair, he wore a hat big enough to sag over his ears. His foot gear was held together by loops of wire with the ends twisted together, his baggy trousers were held up by a frayed length of cotton rope, and his wool shirt had long ago lost its bone buttons.

Ty spoke to him. He gave the kid a run-down of what was expected of him if he came to work on the Circle L. The hours were long, the work hard.

He emphasized one drawback unique to ranch life. This rolling prairie land, an ancient buffalo pasture, was fine country for running cattle and raising horses, but the remote location took a toll on two-legged critters. In his years of experience he had seen solitude wear on men in various ways. If the kid could not adapt to life in the wide open spaces, or if he could not get along with the crew, then he would have to draw his time.

"Some gents can't hold their tempers," Ty said. "I'll give a man a second chance if I think he deserves it. But if hoo-rawin' comes to bare knuckles, I don't give a damn who started it, who's right, who's wrong. Anyone who fights is sent packing. Understand?"

Staring down at worn-out boots, the kid mumbled a promise to get along with the crew. Ty glanced at Sheriff Rogers and nodded once.

"Obliged," the lawman said. Lifting his hand to his hat brim in a parting gesture, he turned and left the saloon.

The ramrod turned his attention to the kid. "I'll get you outfitted on my line of credit at the mercantile, but the money's coming out of your pay. You'll need a couple months to work off the debt, and, believe me, you will work. Understand?"

Eyes still downcast, the kid mumbled: "Yeah."

A bloodless scalping took place in the tonsorial parlor that day. After the shearing came a hot soak in a tub in the back room. Ty noted the kid's swollen forearm and a dark bruise marking the spot where the brakeman had struck him.

"Your arm busted?"

The kid answered with a shake of his head. He slid the arm into murky water.

"Stick it out," Ty said. "Stick your arm out straight out where I can see it."

The kid shook his head.

"Do as I say, son," Ty said, "or we're not gonna get along."

The kid slowly raised his arm out of the soapy bath water. He extended it to full length.

"Wiggle your fingers," Ty said.

He grimaced, but moved his fingers freely.

Satisfied, Ty said: "All right. You're working for me now."

The kid followed Ty to the Coalton Mercantile. He entered the store clothed in filthy, high-smelling rags, and came out sporting stiff duds, a stockman's hat that fit a shorn head, and new boots. Wrapped in store paper and secured by string, spare clothing and underwear were tucked under his good arm. From the look of him, the kid was ready to go to work. Whether he would deliver on a promise was the unanswered question.

The kid was ready to eat. No question about that. He did not miss a meal after Ty brought him to the home ranch. Far from it. He ate supper like a bear coming out of a winter den. Breakfast was wolfed down as though starvation stalked him. Midday, whether the grub was camp fare of fried sow-belly and biscuits coated in oily gravy, or the standard mess-hall slop of spuds with a carrot-and-turnip mix heaped over stringy cuts of beefsteak—the kid eyed the chow platter like a predator closing in on prey.

Drawing his sheathed knife with a deliberation that was worrisome, he slowly wiped the flat of the blade on his trouser leg. The moment that platter came in reach, he lit into the beefsteak, sore arm notwithstanding. Stabbing, sawing, slicing, slashing, he cut and chewed in a wordless forcefulness that cast a pall over the ranch hands taking their repast in the mess hall. The ranch cook, Cornelius, looked on in ill-disguised disgust. They had all seen the kid chow down. The ferocity of his attack unfolded with all of the fascination of a scheduled train wreck. Hunched over their plates on the long table, ranch hands cast sidelong glances at him while awaiting the finale.

They were not disappointed. After mopping his plate with a soda biscuit, the kid stuffed the soggy bread into his mouth. Beardless cheeks bulged when a rumbling belch blew his mouth open, spraying biscuit crumbs across the width of the table. After one more belch, he wiped the back of his hand on his mouth and stood.

Corny retreated before him as the kid sheathed his knife on his way out of the mess hall. The back door slammed shut. Cowhands raised their gazes from tin plates, and conversation picked up a bit.

"I'm a-telling you," Bill Connors said ominously.

Smitty Reeves grinned. "A-telling us what, ol' hoss?"

"Why, that kid," Bill replied, gesturing to the door. "The night hawk."

The moniker "night hawk" had been bestowed on him by the Circle L riders. With no other name offered, and with the kid's propensity for working in the horse barn by lantern light, the job title was a nickname that stuck.

Corny asked now: "What about him, Bill?"

A walrus mustache and drooping eyelids lent a perpetually mournful expression to Bill's face. "Why, he must have a tapeworm living in his gut, the way he eats. I'm a-telling you. It ain't natural."

Court O'Hara ran a hand through his tousled red hair. "A wee bit hungry even for a growing lad, now, isn't he?"

Lanky Dean Bowles gripped a knife as he studiously sawed meat on a dented plate. "Hate to think what he's growing into," he muttered without looking up from his labor.

"All I know is," Bill went on, "it ain't natural for a kid to pack away grub like he does. Huh, Smitty?" He looked to his saddle partner for confirmation.

Smitty masticated while he cogitated. He was a man who prided himself on his ability to consider all angles and examine every nuance before stating his views on the bunkhouse debate of the day. As such discussions went among the men, this one was a lightweight. He readily summed it all up when he spoke around a mouthful of gristle.

"What the hell is natural about that night hawk, anyhow?"

Until he wised up to pranks and fool's errands, the kid was sent to a shed or the tack room in the horse barn on such pretenses as fetching a can of striped paint, a board stretcher, a pine knot extractor, or a square nail sharpener. If he could not locate such a tool, he was to find Mr. Johnson and ask him where it was. He was reminded to remove his hat out of respect for the foreman's exalted station, too.

By the time his bruised arm healed, the kid was worn to a nub. He worked all the time. Wrangler duties by day spilled over to the chores of the ranch night hawk after sunset. Under the heavy-handed tutelage of Ty Johnson, the seam between those jobs was invisible. Endless chores ran together, endlessly.

Fed up, the kid raised that issue with the ramrod. "Working two jobs like you got me doing, my pay oughta be doubled up."

"Which one of those jokesters put that bee in your ear?" Ty asked with a grin. "Whoever it is, go tell him you need a can of polka dot paint."

The kid was not laughing. Never caught up with his work, one completed task only led to another chore. From sunup to sundown there was always more work than daylight. This was true whether the tasks at hand amounted to routine jobs such as driving the wagon to the foothills of the Cheyenne Mountains where he bucked downed timber, sawed sections and split them, or field-dressed a deer carcass for Corny to butcher and salt down. When range riders departed to make a gather and move a herd to new pasture, the kid was left behind—another point of contention between the ramrod and the night hawk.

In cattle country herds were frequently moved from one sector of the ranch to another as a means of preventing over-grazing and the erosion of top soil. Come autumn, three-year-old steers were rounded up by riders on the Circle L. Neighboring spreads did the same—Pete Spencer and his Bar S down south, Josh Evans and his Lazy E out east, and Henry Spotswood and his Turtle brand to the west of the Circle L boundary. At their annual roundups, a man from each ranch kept a tally of branded steers and sale horses. Livestock that had wandered off their ranges were bunched and driven back to their home ranches.

On the Circle L, Ty always made the final count himself before livestock was driven to the railroad siding some forty miles away from ranch headquarters. Every year he confirmed totals in the Coalton pens, using a pencil stub to mark a sheet of lined paper he had ripped from a ledger.

After negotiations via telegraph with Chicago reps, a year's profit was calculated. Operating cash was deposited in the First National Bank of Coalton. The balance was transferred by wire to the account of Major Gregory Lange in Whitmoor, Maryland. Lange, residing half a continent away from the Colorado prairie, was the absentee owner of the Circle L.

While the riders did their work, the kid swatted horseflies and slapped mosquitoes as he mucked out stalls in the cavernous barn, split wood for the cook's stove fire, and hauled water by the bucket from the pump. Above all, come hell or no water, the remuda had to be ready. Ty pounded that into him. Saddle horses were to be hazed out of the fenced pasture and corralled at first light, the mounts rested and gear ready for the cowhands—six days a week, Sundays as needed.

It was not fair, not a lick. Nobody argued the point, but when the kid cursed within Ty's hearing, he learned where that got him.

Pissing and moaning about working all day and half the damned night to corral saddle mounts and repair tack for the men who leisurely picked their damned teeth like the king's princes after a breakfast of eggs and summer sausage with fresh-baked bread slathered in butter and honey, and hot coffee—the damned injustice of it all brought anger and muttered curses from the kid. It was the swearing that earned him one newly minted take-it-or-leave-it from the ramrod.

"Son, if you aim to cuss," Ty said, "go out behind the barn and let her rip. Just don't do it where I can hear you."

The night hawk glowered. His face was reddened, marked by mosquito stings and horsefly bites, bleeding where he scratched his skin.

"Follow orders, do your work, don't cuss. Understand?"

Tyler Johnson did not rule by his fists. He was slender with fine features and a close shave. Possessing an air of authority, he left no doubt who was in charge and that he expected men to obey him. A whispered curse signaled defiance, and Ty had learned a long time ago to nip it in the bud. One ranch hand swearing under his breath was guilty of more than an utterance of pain or frustration. Cursing was a challenge to the ramrod's rule. If ignored, other men would take it up, and in time whispered oaths would be directed at Ty, undermining his authority. Authority once lost, he believed, could never be regained.

"I oughta quit you," the kid said now.

Ty studied him. "Quitting gets to be a bad habit, son. Besides, you owe me. Two months' wages for duds. Remember?"

Still glowering, the kid did not acknowledge that point.

"If you stick," Ty said, "you'll have all winter to tend critters, buck snow, haul hay, and catch up on your sleep. Now, grab a shovel."

The kid hesitated again, a gesture that could have been taken for an act of defiance—or as the second part of *take-it-or-leave-it*.

"Get moving on my say-so," Ty said in a measured tone.

The kid found the better part of valor was to shut his

trap and take up the shovel. Even though angered, he was resigned to grudging obedience. In truth, he knew he had no choice. With his debt to the Circle L, and without a horse and saddle to his name, he had nowhere to go or any way to get there.

At once, though, he was edgy and impatient, frustrated by the turtle-slow pace of his life. Like any kid hung up halfway between boyhood and manhood, he yearned to be free. He sought the freedom to come and go as he pleased, and craved the latitude to live on his own terms. Exactly how to achieve those goals was less clear in his mind.

Hunger pangs stayed with him, and sharp-edged memories cut deep. He was beset with dreams so vivid that he sometimes awoke with a start, convinced he had smelled steak slapped into a hot fry pan, convinced he had heard the pop and sizzle of meat cooking, convinced until he awakened to the rasping snores of men asleep in the bunkhouse. Those sounds and odors reminded him where he was.

Chapter Two

Like a stilled sea, the rolling grasslands of northern Colorado stretched out in swells and heaves as far as the eye could reach. Nearly treeless, the great plain was cut by ravines and etched with gullies. Vast herds of buffalo native to this land were consigned to the ages, but their wallows still seeped water in the withering heat of summer and in winter the terrain provided shelter from blue northers.

Aside from wolves taking calves, or the occasional mortal injury suffered by an animal, Circle L livestock flourished. Branded cattle ranged in open prairie while the ranch's horse herd was held in fenced pastures. Blanketed with grama and buffalo grass, this land was trimmed with pear cactus, rabbitbrush, and sage.

Corny's hand-watered vegetables were fenced with chicken wire to guard against forays by rabbits and deer. In constant struggles ranging from hot winds to gully-washers, the thin soil of the region barely sustained his straw-mulched garden plots.

The early morning chill in the air signaled the coming change of seasons. Free ranging steers followed their instincts and held to the lee side of foothills. Forested slopes stacked against distant peaks, so named for the Cheyenne tribe, and that was where Circle L riders cut sign. The imprints of small hoofs indicated pintos—so-called "Indian ponies"—were on the loose in range land claimed by the Circle L.

In the bunkhouse after supper Ty joined the ranch hands. The men pulled away from dominos and checker matches and set aside back issues of the *Police Gazette*, *Velvet Vice*, and *Rocky Mountain News*. The ramrod discussed the favored topic—horses.

The tracks were of interest. For among these men, paints were considered to be inferior to "American" horses. Crossbreeding was believed to be detrimental to the well-being of the herd. Offered as proof, pintos were undersized, said to be weakened by centuries of random inbreeding.

The kid reclined on his bunk, listening. Other than an indifferent shrug, he offered no opinion when Ty asked what he thought of the effects of inbreeding among bands of wild horses.

Ty eyed him. He recalled the kid's claim in Coalton, a boast about handling horses. So far, the kid had demonstrated a rudimentary ability to wave his hat and drive saddle mounts from a pasture to the corral every morning, and back again in the evening after sunset.

Smitty and Bill consulted the ramrod. And, at dawn, the pair made a hard ride from the ranch headquarters. On the third day out, they picked up the tracks of unshod horses. On the fourth day a dust cloud revealed the location of the herd. After a brief pursuit they closed in on a band of wild horses. Most of them were pintos, small in stature and splotched in coloration, but several were American stock. A big black and white stallion, the riders' quarry, was in the lead, tail up and mane flying in full gallop.

"Strap wings on that big bastard," Bill said, "and he'll fly."

Smitty nodded in silent agreement.

Struck by their close-up view of Domino, as Circle L riders called him, Smitty and Bill glimpsed a dim scar on the stallion's shoulder. The distance was too great and the horse too fast for either of them to read the brand.

Fleet and smart, the stallion had run off contenders and captured half a dozen mares from a pasture where a section of wire fence was down. This lightning-swift raid was cited as evidence to prove a theory circulating among ranchers. Even though tamed, the theory went, a saddle horse will answer a primitive call and revert to a wild state if given half a chance.

Ty believed it. He had lost good horses to that stallion. He figured Domino had leaned against a fence post until it snapped. With such thievery in mind, Ty had placed a bounty on him.

"Bring that big son-of-a-bitch in," was the order from the ramrod. He added: "If you can't get a rope on him, shoot him."

In addition, Ty had offered a reward of $2 for every outlaw horse the ranch hands managed to haze into a Circle L corral, pinto or otherwise. He had a plan in mind. Spotted ponies, if captured, would be "roped, rode, and sold" in the Coalton livery. Larger horses with solid coloring would be kept on the ranch to fill out the remuda.

Now Smitty and Bill gazed at broomtails on the run, admiring their wild grace. Domino circled his harem and, like any good general, protected the rear. The stallion halted and faced the intruders. With a toss of his head and shake of his mane, he bluffed a charge. Then he reared, pawing the sky.

The two cowhands reined their own mounts down at this challenge and show of power. Exchanging a glance, they grinned. Their thoughts needed no voice. Each knew what the other was thinking. The rifle in Smitty's saddle boot was a compact, lever-action .30-30 Winchester carbine. Bill packed a long-barreled Remington, a bolt-action .30-06. From this distance he had the best chance of bringing the big stallion down, or at least slowing him with a bullet to that muscular body.

When the moment came, though, neither man reached for his rifle. As Ty well knew, gunning down a good horse, even an outlaw stallion wreaking havoc, was abhorrent to men who earned their keep in the saddle. This pair of ranch hands pulled makings from vest pockets, rolled smokes, sealed them, and lit up. They figured Ty had not seriously expected them to shoot the stallion, that he had only expressed frustration after being outsmarted by a horse.

Saddle leather creaked while they smoked and observed the milling herd of wild ponies. Smitty made a quick tally—twenty-six. Prairie survivors, these diminutive horses were strong and spirited. If bloodlines could be traced, Smitty counted himself among those who believed the ponies would be proven to be related to runaways from the remuda of Hernando Cortés himself, that their Spanish progeny, born of Arabians, had run free for three centuries in North America.

Smitty and Bill exchanged a nod. They ground out their cigarettes. Tugging hat brims down a notch, they kicked their mounts and came at the horse herd on the run. Flanked, Domino wheeled and fled. His band followed. Colts and fillies leaped in youthful exuberance as they made tentative efforts to find their own paths before rejoining the fleeing herd.

The two cowhands managed to cut a dapple-gray mare and her snow-white filly from the harem. The mare caught their eye. She had some size to her, and her coat shone like satin. If Domino had sired her filly, it was a safe bet the offspring possessed strong bloodlines. The two riders hazed her and kept her under control by roping her foal. Alternately dragged with head bobbing and high-stepping across the prairie, where the filly went, mama was not far behind.

Arriving at the home ranch, the mare followed her prancing foal into the corral. She frantically circled the snubbing post and crashed against the rails when she figured out the gate had closed behind her.

In answer to the ruckus, ranch hands left the bunkhouse to look over this spirited mare and her foal. The night hawk followed, head downcast in a sullen pose. Without being told, he grabbed the reins of both Circle L saddle horses. He led them into the barn where he would strip them, wipe them down, and turn them out to pasture with a ration of grain.

In the meantime, Ty had stepped out on the verandah of the ranch house. He greeted Smitty and Bill with mugs of coffee—a dark brew discretely spiked with shots of rye. They drank while recounting their sighting of wild ponies. As for tossing a loop on Domino, Smitty freely admitted he'd sooner rope a cyclone. Bill hemmed and hawed, finally claiming they never got close enough to Domino for a clean shot.

Ty accepted the tale with a nod and asked no more questions. When the kid returned, Ty jerked his thumb at the mare.

"She's yours, son," he said, "if you can get a halter on her."

The kid turned. He eyed the mare while the ramrod

crossed the porch to a wicker armchair and lowered himself into it.

Reaching into an empty horseshoe nail keg beside the chair, Ty took out a buckskin tobacco pouch and his pipe. As he methodically filled the bowl of the meerschaum, his eyes were fixed on the kid. He tamped Prince Albert to the proper density with his index finger. Firing the tobacco, then, he drew on it and exhaled a cloud of smoke.

Word spread as the kid moved to the corral. Two more Circle L ranch hands, Clyde Rand and George Taylor, drifted in from the bunkhouse. Last, Corny thumbed chaw into his mouth as he joined them from the cook shack.

The cowhands leaned on the top rail of the corral to watch. Constructed of slender lodgepole pines, the top rail was worn smooth, smooth as a schoolmarm's leg, as the men put it.

Under the glare of their stares, the kid hesitated. He glanced their way. Some onlookers were bareheaded while others had shoved sweat-rimmed hats up on white foreheads. All of them looked on with expectant expressions lining their faces, brows arched. Even Bill's mournful demeanor was not so much bloodhound-sad now as it was a look of interest to see what would happen next.

The kid bent down. He ducked between the second and third rails as he entered the corral. Whinnying, the mare turned to face him. At once, her foal was determined to nurse.

The kid's gaze drifted to a coiled rope on the corral post anchoring the gate. Squaring his shoulders, he strode to it in long, purposeful strides. He grabbed the rope off the post. Then he turned and approached the mare while feeding out enough slack to make a loop. He had seen cowhands rope their saddle mounts before laying on a clean, dry saddle blanket, and now he emulated their technique. *What the hell does the night hawk think he's doing?* was the unspoken question among onlookers.

Several men glanced uneasily at the ramrod. No one spoke. As long as Ty sat up there on the verandah silently observing goings-on while smoking his pipe, none of the men would make a move to assist the night hawk. Clearly Ty had something in mind.

The kid's daily chore of hazing saddle mounts to and from the horse pasture was routine, but not always an easy task. As the itinerant horse doctor was fond of saying: Some horses are less unco-operative than others. The kid was sometimes kicked, occasionally bitten, nearly always bumped around by unco-operative jugheads. None of these experiences prepared him for gentling down a wild horse— particularly a mare protecting her nursing offspring.

When the kid drew close, the filly panicked and pranced on spindly legs. Whinnying again, the mare let him know he was too close. She charged, bucking and rearing, with hoofs lashing out.

The kid turned and ran clumsily, drawing guffaws from the rail birds for beating a hasty retreat. In the next moment the ranch hands were silenced when the kid's new boots tangled in the rope. Arms wind-milling, he fell headlong. He landed face down hard enough to bloody his own nose. Sprawled in a puddle of horse piss, he rolled in crusted mud and entangled himself in the rope as he tried to escape.

The mare charged again. This time she got a hoof into him. The kid cried out, grabbing his side where he had been kicked. Grimacing, he wiped his nose and looked in alarm at a smear of blood on his hand.

The mare came for him again. Clawing dirt, the kid shed the rope and crabbed his way to safety under the bottom rail. Outside the corral he lay on the ground, gasping, as he bled from one nostril. Raising up to his knees, the kid wiped his nose and examined the smear of blood on the back of his hand.

"This here night hawk," Bill announced loud enough for all to hear, "he don't know shit about horses."

Smitty thought about that. "Gotta give him a wad of credit, though, Bill."

"For what?" Bill demanded.

"Why, for roping himself," Smitty replied.

"Huh?"

"He roped and throwed himself," Smitty explained, "like a yearling ready for a hot branding iron. Ever seen such a thing?"

"When you put it thataway," Bill allowed, "can't say I have."

The cowhands chuckled as the kid got to his feet. He staggered to the horse trough, bent over it, and submerged his head in the water. He came up blowing, and vigorously wiped his face with both hands. Blood trickled out of the one nostril as he turned to face his tormentors.

"Someday . . . you won't . . . you won't . . . do . . . no laughing . . . not at me, you won't . . . be laughing no more. . . ."

Bill taunted him. "What day of the week is that, night hawk?"

The kid glowered.

"I want to know," Bill went on, "so I can be there to see it."

The kid cast a go-to-hell look at him.

Ty observed them from the wicker armchair on the verandah. He smoked his pipe until the kid turned and walked away from the corral. Lunging to his feet, Ty yanked the pipe from his mouth and rushed to the edge of the verandah.

"Pick up that rope!" he shouted.

Halting at the sound of the ramrod's booming voice, the kid turned. His mystified gaze swung from the verandah to the corral where the tangled rope lay in dirt and manure.

"That's Kentucky hemp," Ty said. "Don't you ever walk off and leave a good rope on the ground like that. Pick it up. Go on. Pick it up and wipe the crap off. Wipe it good. Coil it up and put it back on that post. Put it back where it belongs . . . just like you found it."

When the kid seemed rooted in wordless silence, Ty shouted: "Go on! Get after it!"

The kid attempted to throw a silent curse at him, but from the ranch house verandah Ty stared him down. Smoke drifted from the bowl of his meerschaum after he thrust the pipe into his mouth and drew on it, jaw jutting.

The kid backtracked. He paused at the rail. Ducking into the corral, he eyed the mare and her foal. He snatched up the rope and warily backed away. Outside the corral he wiped off mud and manure, coiled the rope, and put it back on the post. Without so much as a glance back at Ty, the kid headed for the bunkhouse, trailing after riders drifting to the door.

In preparation for fall roundup on the Circle L, triple-wintered steers were cut from the herds. To find them, riders ranged across the prairie in pairs. They searched far-flung gullies, water holes, and favorite hiding places to root out the critters.

The nature of the annual gather made it impractical to load up the chuck wagon and take Corny with them. The ranch cook issued canteens and tins from his well-stocked pantry, outfitting each set of saddlebags with rations for eight days. Tobacco and spirits and necessary gear came from the cowhands' own war bags.

Horses prancing and snorting, the riders cantered out of the corral at dawn. Clyde Rand and George Taylor headed west while Court O'Hara and Dean Bowles peeled off to cover the south sector of the ranch. Mike Benning and Dick Hayes rode eastward. Smitty and Bill angled toward the northern boundary bumping up against the Wyoming line. As for Ty, he would cover all points of the compass to make a preliminary count and see for himself how the gather was shaping up this year.

Privately the kid asked Ty to let him ride with him. He had obviously been mulling this request, for he made his case in a practiced tone of voice. He reminded Ty a spare saddle was in the barn, and he identified one of the Circle L horses, a roan gelding with some miles behind him, as a gentle mount, easy to handle.

The ramrod did not disagree, but he answered with a shake of his head. The kid stiffened, jaw set as he waited for an explanation. True, the saddle was there, and true, the gelding was as tame as a house cat. Even so, Ty ordered the kid to stay behind with Corny. While the riders were gone, the two of them would swamp out the mess hall and scrub the kitchen—top to bottom, wall to wall—and apply a coat of whitewash to the weathered boards of the outbuildings.

Anger flaring, the kid answered with a curse. "God damn it!"

"What did I tell you about that kind of talk?" Ty asked.

"I don't care what you said!" the kid shouted. "You're making me mad! Mad as hell!"

Ty eyed him. "Doesn't take much, does it?"

The kid drew a ragged breath. "How'd you feel, cooped

up here like a damned dog? You won't let me ride, you won't let me do nothing . . . nothing except damn' near get myself killed by a wild horse. How the hell am I gonna get any god-damned experience if you won't let me ride with the hands?"

"You told Sheriff Rogers you had experience handling horses," Ty reminded him.

His youthful face flushed, the kid spat on the ground between them. "You and that sheriff can go to hell!"

"When you start acting like a man," Ty said evenly, "you'll ride with men."

The kid spun away. Kicking a clod of dirt into a cloud of dust, he headed to the cook shack for his next set of chores. Corny did not want him around, but Ty had ordered him to put the kid to work and supervise him. The cook eyed a $10 bonus in the form of a gold eagle, grimaced, and snatched the bribe from Ty's hand.

More than ever, Ty was convinced this green kid lacked not only the skills, but the patience and common sense required to handle a horse and to herd livestock in open country. It was dangerous work, and Ty figured it was safer for man and beast alike for the kid to be occupied with routine chores from dark to dark on the home place.

The plan for roundup directed Circle L riders to bunch the steers and drive them to one prominent landmark, a granite uplift known to them as Ty's Bluff. Feldspar gave the massive stone formation a reddish cast. With a year-around spring trickling into grass-ringed ponds, the bluff was a natural formation well suited for holding cattle.

Riders would head up three-year-olds and drive them from Ty's Bluff to a pasture near ranch headquarters. From there, the next leg of the journey was the drive to steel at Coalton. Then it was a matter of waiting for the U.P. to deliver the rolling stock Ty had ordered. When the cattle cars were positioned on the siding, Circle L riders would push steers from holding pens through slanted chutes into each car.

Smitty Reeves and Bill Connors probed draws in the foothills. They ranged northward, farther than ever before. Most gulches were bone dry. They were surprised to come upon a wide valley that bore a seep. The wetland backed up enough water to nurture cat-tails and an expanse of native grasses for several hundred acres by a ranch hand's estimate. On the far side stood the tumble-down remains of a homesteader's cabin. With a sod roof caved in, the logs were cracked and weathered to the gray-brown hues of the prairie. Horned buffalo skulls, sun-bleached and gnawed by rodents, lay scattered on the ground nearby.

As they circled the marsh, Smitty glimpsed movement in the willows. In the next instant a steer erupted from a thicket. The critter was not alone. Spooked, others charged out, startling men and mounts.

With both horses rearing, their riders grabbed saddle horns and held on for dear life. By the time the exhibition of bucking and sun-fishing was over, Smitty and Bill had flushed fourteen steers out of the brush—big bruisers, every one. All wore the Circle L brand, an indication the bunch had been missed by last year's crew. They may have been missed by riders assigned here two seasons past, as well. If so, these critters would be five years old, perhaps six.

"Damned if this here sight don't make a man crave his own spread," Bill said solemnly. "Look at it. I'd sure take this one."

Smitty followed his partner's gaze sweeping over terrain lush with vegetation. The northern exposure was banked by a stone-crested ridge. A large herd could survive here year around.

Smitty and Bill exchanged a glance. Even at top pay, the notion of owning a ranch was a dream, a dream as vivid as it was unattainable on a cowhand's wages.

They admired native grasses growing around the pooling spring. Unlike alkali-crusted seeps common to prairie lands, the water here was sweet, diamond clear. Myriad tracks of birds and small animals were imprinted in soft ground like the letters of a lost alphabet. Bigger tracks told a different story. This pocket valley where grass stood knee-high to a tall man was a refuge that had nurtured a variety of wild-life—pronghorn, deer, elk, buffalo, cougars, wolves, jack rabbits, great blue herons, hawks, geese, and wild ducks—for untold centuries.

Steers had been brought here by men. So had the horses to herd them.

These bruisers, lost for one or two seasons, were range-wise, unaccustomed to hazing by cowhands. Lashings from willow switches made them as irritable as Satan on a good day.

Smitty and Bill succeeded in driving them from familiar terrain, but nearly busted two good cutting horses to get the job done. The prospect of leaving high grass and sweet water simply did not suit the steers. Agile, the big critters kept circling back, headed for home ground at any cost.

Where's that damned night hawk when we need him? became the running joke between Smitty and Bill as they herded unruly steers in the general direction of Ty's Bluff.

"Reckon the night hawk," Smitty said, "could teach these steers a thing or two."

Bill cast a doubtful look at him. "Teach them what?"

"Why, to rope themselves," Smitty replied. "Like the kid

done to himself in the corral."

"Huh?"

"Think on it," Smitty went on. "A whole herd of steers roping themselves, purty as you please." He paused. "Hell, I reckon the night hawk could teach one to brand the others, too. A couple fine gents like us, all we gotta do is stoke up a branding fire and sit back and watch."

Bill added: "And collect our danged pay."

"Hell, yes," Smitty said.

A whitefaced steer wheeled and suddenly butted Bill's mount, hitting him squarely on the shoulder. The horse staggered and reared.

Smitty was not surprised to see his partner tumble out of the saddle. Ain't a horse that can't be rode, according to the old saw, ain't a buckaroo that can't be throwed. Both of them had been thrown many times.

Smitty thought about that as his partner cart-wheeled out of the saddle and landed in the dirt, headfirst.

Riderless, Bill's cow horse limped away with reins trailing. Instead of jumping up to slap dust-laden clothing and chase after his mount, Bill lay on the ground, unmoving, his head twisted away from his upper body.

Smitty kicked out of the stirrups. He threw a leg over the horn and slid to the ground. Dry soil cascaded before the thrust of his boots as he ran. Suddenly light-headed, he reeled. The day was not cold, but a chill cut through him.

He sprinted around sagebrush and leaped over clumps of pear cactus. Reaching the still form on the ground, he wanted to believe Bill had been knocked unconscious, the usual outcome of a cowhand bucked out of his saddle.

Yet at once Smitty knew the truth. A sob wracked him. He wept as he drew up beside the motionless figure. Dropping to chaps-covered knees, he stared through his tears, stared at unblinking eyes in a stilled face.

Smitty reached out. His rough hand stroked the man's broad forehead, the skin pale where it had been shielded from the sun by a full-brimmed stockman's hat. Rocked by grief, Smitty withdrew his hand. Still he stared, his sense of disbelief overwhelmed by awful reality. If there had been any doubt moments ago, there could be none now. Bill Connors was dead, his neck broken on impact when he hit the ground.

Chapter Three

Ty was not a man to believe in anything he could not see or grab. He was distrustful of intuition—his or anyone else's—but, when Smitty and Bill failed to arrive at the bluff two days after he expected them, premonition settled over him like a leaden cloud. Those two men were as dependable as sunrise. Concerned for their safety, Ty was determined to settle his mind about their whereabouts.

Circle L riders offered to join him in the sweep of a wide-ranging search. Ty declined their offers. He figured he could find the pair, and instructed his men to bunch the steers according to plan and drive them to the pasture near the home ranch. By then Ty hoped to have found Smitty and Bill, and the three of them would catch up.

Ty saddled up. He set out at a fast trot, heading due north. At nightfall he made a cold camp under a starry sky, slept fitfully while owls hooted and coyotes yelped and barked, and hit the saddle again at first light. The day passed with the horse crossing dry flats and dropping into arroyos. By the second night, doubts coursed through Ty's thoughts as the futility of this search grew in his mind.

He felt a measure of regret for sending all the riders to

the home place with market-ready steers. At the time he had made that decision, he had thought the most important thing was to keep the herd together. Now he scanned the horizon, wishing he had brought half a dozen men with him. As never before, he knew the north sector of the ranch covered a whole lot of ground. And the fact was he was relying on dumb luck to cut Smitty and Bill's trail—dumb luck and gunshots. He could only hope to stumble across a campsite and pick up the tracks of shod hoofs, or hear the report of a gun to guide his search.

With the latter in mind, he drew his Colt. Cocking the single-action revolver, he pointed it skyward. He held a tight rein as he pulled the trigger. The six-shooter bucked in his hand, gunsmoke plumed, and the gelding pranced as the loud report reverberated through a silent land. The shot went unanswered.

In the morning, Ty angled north toward the Wyoming line. He watched the horizon for a dust cloud and studied the dry soil in search of tracks. He found pronghorn and jack rabbits. No sign of shod horses, or Domino and his band of wild ponies, either.

Amid the long shadows of late afternoon he fired his Colt again. Other than scaring birds, that shot went unanswered, too. Then at dusk a bitter scent of burning sage reached him. His horse tossed his head and pranced. Unable to find the source, Ty fired his pistol again.

This time he heard the deep *boom* of a rifle shot. The sound of the heavy weapon rumbled across the prairie like distant thunder. That shot was followed by two more in quick succession—a signal for help.

Ty spurred his horse toward the reports. The pungent odor of burning sage intensified. In gathering darkness he spotted a glow from leaping flames, a fire too large for an ordinary campsite. Drawing closer, he saw a bonfire on the crest of a hill.

Ty peered ahead. Someone was up there, someone who had dragged clumps of sagebrush to the hilltop and set them aflame. Now fire shadows played across a lanky figure. No two men strike the same posture, and even from a distance, in failing light, Ty recognized this one.

"Smitty!"

The cowhand stood with a long-barreled rifle cradled in the crook of one arm. Ty recognized the big Remington owned by Bill, and wondered why Smitty held it. He called out again as he urged his horse upslope.

"Smitty! What the hell happened?"

The cowhand shifted the rifle from one arm to the other. He offered no reply until Ty topped the hill where the fire blazed.

"Bill. . . ." Smitty's voice trailed off.

"Where is he?" Ty asked, drawing rein.

"Dead."

For a long moment neither man moved. In the vast silence of a prairie evening saddle leather creaked and burning sage crackled. *Dead.* The reality of death, the suddenness and finality of it, left him stunned. Ty's gaze went to a sougan spread on the ground. Dusty, scuffed boots with pointed toes protruded from one end of the blanket.

"Bill?" he asked needlessly.

Smitty nodded.

"What . . . what happened?"

"Throwed."

Ty shook himself as though awakening. He grabbed the saddle horn and swung down. Pulling off his hat, he stood over the covered body, head bowed in reverential silence. Then he knelt. He reached out and grasped a corner of the sougan. When he raised it, firelight exposed the beard-stumbled face of Bill, a rugged expression in repose, a face at once familiar and strange.

Ty looked up at Smitty. Expression dulled, the cowhand turned away to stare into gathering darkness. His jaw was streaked with campfire ash where he had rubbed tears away. Ty lowered the blanket and stood. He looked at Smitty. These two men had been close. He recalled seeing them ride out of the corral, side-by-side, two ranch hands who worked in unison with scarcely a word or motion wasted between them.

In a halting voice now, Smitty recounted their discovery of a marsh and the cache of Circle L steers. He described the sudden charge from one bruiser that had spilled Bill out of his saddle.

Ty looked around. "Where's the cutting horse?"

Smitty gestured to night shadows filling the arroyo behind them. "Over yonder somewhere. That jughead kept shying and hopping away from me." He added: "Sounds loco, Ty, but it seemed like that horse knew Bill was dead."

Ty did not argue the point.

Smitty fell silent before continuing. "Hell, Ty, I didn't know what to do . . . I couldn't just leave him here . . . couldn't just cover him with his sougan and throw dirt over him . . . couldn't . . . couldn't leave him to the coyotes."

Jaw clenched, Ty battled his emotions.

"Figured you'd send some of the boys," Smitty went on, "and I figured somebody would see my signal fire. I heard your gunshot and answered with three from Bill's rifle. It's louder than my carbine. Then I seen you coming, riding out of the dusk like something from the spirit world. . . ."

Smitty's voice trailed off again as burning sagebrush popped and crackled, sending off flares and puffs of smoke.

Ty pushed his hat up on his forehead. More than fatigue from his search, grief weighed on him. He drew a deep breath. It all seemed unreal, the crackling fire in gathering darkness where a sougan covered the corpse—yet at once the death of Bill Connors was all too real.

"Come morning," Ty said, "we'll catch that horse . . . carry Bill's remains to the home place . . . nail up a pine box, six-by-three . . . dig a grave . . . say some words over him . . . a proper burying."

Smitty nodded in mute reply.

"Where's his kin?" Ty asked.

Smitty's brow furrowed. "Bill never talked of his back trail. Not to me."

Ty eyed the cowhand. The face he saw glistened where the wavering light of flames reflected tears. He reached out and draped a hand over his shoulder.

"You did the right thing, Smitty. Don't ever forget that."

Accounts of half-wild steers on the prod and the violent death of a good man on the lone prairie did not reach the ears of Major Gregory Lange. Half a continent away, the absentee owner of the Circle L resided in his family's estate in Maryland. Lange rightly claimed ownership of the ranch in Colorado, but he was largely unaware of the gritty details and daily dangers encountered by men working cattle from horseback on the prairie.

Major Lange was born into a life of ease. Ample meals were set before him on French linen with silver service, English china, and Irish crystal. Awaiting him every morning, his tailored clothing was freshly laundered and pressed, his dress shoes and riding boots polished, hats brushed, gloves cleaned—all of these labors performed by squads of servants and caretakers answering his beck and call. So it was he grew to manhood in the lavish confines of a columned mansion, a residence that was imposing even by local standards of vast wealth.

Constructed of cloud-white marble shipped from Carrara, Italy, Major Lange's father had commissioned his version of an American Parthenon. The estate was fronted by a line of towering Doric columns. The original was a masterpiece of Greek architecture, and Roman builders of Antiquity would not be the last to imitate it. In North America of the 19th Century, captains of industry—those ambitious robber barons with their unbridled appetites—constructed their own monuments to money modeled on the classical Greek style.

Known locally as "the Lange estate", the marble structure commanded a grassy knoll like a white-iced cake centered on a bride's lace tablecloth. The knoll overlooked the blue waters of Chesapeake Bay. The estate itself was set off by manicured hedges, trimmed shrubs, cropped lawns, and the formal gardens admired throughout Whitmoor, Maryland and beyond.

But for carriage trips to Baltimore, Washington, and Richmond with his father, Major Lange had never set foot west of the upper reaches of the James River, a waterway coursing past Maryland's eastern shore. Upon the death of his father, a graveside promise to his mother would hold him there longer.

"Dearest, I cannot bear to be alone. I simply cannot bear it. Don't leave me. Ever. You must promise me that, my dear son."

Frail in physique and aged in her demeanor, Margaret Payson Lange was a woman of mighty resolve. She exacted that promise from her only child in a Sunday visit to her husband's grave, a site framed in wrought iron overlooking the Lange estate and the bay.

Major Lange uttered his promise for her comfort and peace of mind. A lifelong bachelor, he kept his word even as years dragged through one decade and into another. In his own way, he came to a reckoning, alarming as it was. That solemn promise to his mother was not her deathwatch. It was his. For in her dotage, Margaret Payson Lange engaged in a contest of wills, a competition to determine who would expire first, mother or son, and it appeared to him that she drew strength from time's inexorable passage.

In the meantime, Major Lange boasted of his ownership of a cattle ranch out West, and offered a romantic portrayal of the wilds of Colorado where cattle grew large and wild horses ran free. Whether it was a meeting or a social gathering with spirited croquet matches and lawn-bowling contests, Major Lange told all who would listen about his ranch, as though that manly endeavor compensated for the apron strings binding him fast to his mother. His descriptions of the ranch were at once vague and fanciful, the details inconsistent. Listeners nodded politely when he spoke of "my ranch out West in a wild land far beyond the banks of the great Missouri River."

Major Lange was aware of their skepticism. Family friends cast knowing glances at one another, allowing his fantasies to go unchallenged. In truth, Major Lange knew as much—or as little—about the Circle L Ranch as Tyler Johnson penned in tersely worded semi-annual reports. In a weather phenomenon unique to the 1880s, blizzards roared through Montana and Wyoming like highballing freight trains. The winter storms took a murderous toll, die-ups sending the price of beef soaring for a decade.

Ill winds blew good fortune to stockmen in northern Colorado. Sheltered by the terrain, Circle L livestock not only survived blue northers, but procreated handsomely. Major Gregory Lange possessed the bank account to prove it. Profit/loss entries favored his ranch. As to the gritty realities of life and death on the spread, though, it was safe to say the Easterner did not know a red-tail hawk from a night hawk.

Major Lange was not alone in his ignorance. This terrain had been largely overlooked even when a second gold rush swept across the plains to a labyrinth of mountain cañons. The region was still described in print back East as "an arid desert", a land characterized by writers as "endless" and "empty" and "barren". Scribes knew no more of the intermountain West than Major Lange knew of the ranch he owned.

Some of that history was a matter of record. The original Circle L land application and documented water rights dated back to July of 1865, three months after the historic signatures in Appomattox Courthouse in Virginia. The first ranch owners were two Civil War veterans who had journeyed to Colorado Territory. They ran cattle and raised horses until a two-year drought drove them out. By the time Major Lange purchased the ranch, other owners had come and gone, and the pair of war veterans had long since crossed the divide to roam sweet pastures of heaven on a favorite horse under a fine saddle.

Sold, resold, and re-resold by land agents from Coalton to Laramie, the ranch property passed through a succession of owners, all of whom promptly went belly up. To a man, they suffered from a disease known out West as "cattlemanitis". In plain English, if the rattlers don't get you, Mr. Cattleman, bone cold winters will. If the cold doesn't do the trick, sir, well, here comes the drought. Haven't had enough? Try a grass fire this year and a flood

43

from snow melt the next. Stand aside, for spring run-off carries ash from distant wildfires, a fine black soot killing trout and ruining water holes miles downstream.

Of all the ways a man can find to go loco, it seemed each owner of this ranch property discovered a new one.

Telegraph wires sang, as folks said, and in time a Coalton land agent represented Major Lange of Whitmoor, Maryland in the purchase of the ranch property in northern Colorado. The agent knew a cowhand who knew a cook who knew a ramrod, and, based on his recommendation, Major Lange hired Tyler Johnson at $60 a month, half again the standard pay.

Communicating by mail and transferring funds by telegraph from the Maryland bank to the Colorado bank, the two men formed a partnership without ever meeting face to face. A good faith agreement was drawn up, and both signed it. Thus, the partnership between Tyler Johnson and Major Gregory Lange was as straightforward as the history of the ranch itself.

With Ty's savvy and Major Lange's cash, a run-down ranch was reborn. The aging barn was rebuilt, the herd stocked, breeding bulls purchased and pastured. Ty hired Cornelius away from another ranch, luring him with a $5 increase in pay.

Riders were interviewed and hired by Ty in Coalton. Saddle mounts were bought at auction from a neighboring cattleman who had gone bust. After tack was purchased from the same gent, two-legged critters were awarded improved living conditions. These improvements came in the form of feather pillows, new cotton mattresses on the bunks, and a washroom in the back where water could be heated for bathing in an iron tub—a luxury that left cowhands on other ranches shaking their heads in envy.

A rodent-infested and lice-laden bunkhouse was fumigated and refurbished. The structure itself, raised on jacks, was shored up by a foundation of stone blocks. This work exposed a warren of mouse borings under the barn, holes that provided a habitat for bull snakes. Left alone to do their work, the silent, slithering serpents feasted on rodents and their attendant fleas. A man might kill a rattler without a thought, but bull snakes were honored guests in their "holey hotel".

Every spring, ranch hands were hired. Through the season, cash bonuses were awarded by discretion of the ramrod. Major Lange paid his employees top dollar, a policy that reaped benefits. Other ranchers contended with drifters who promised to work the season, only to skip out after pay day, many stealing a horse or two by moonlight. Riders for the Circle L were skilled, dependable men who had mastered the craft. They kept their word and they earned their pay. Ty made certain of that.

Come autumn, the ranch hands completed their season when livestock was driven to holding pens at the Coalton siding of the Union Pacific. After steers were loaded into slatted boxcars in a train bound for the Chicago stockyards, the men collected their last pay for the season. Saying their so-longs at the bar in the Comet, then, most headed for home and hearth by rail or by coach, a few on their own mounts to warmer climes where they wintered like migratory critters.

As a man of inherited wealth, Major Lange could afford a streak of eccentricity. That was how ranch hands savvied him. Not that they had ever met. Just as it was common knowledge that Lange had never ventured out West to oversee—or see at all—his holdings, he was said to rely on the expertise of others. Folks knew by way of grapevine that

45

he had been cheated more than once. First skinned in his investment of a nonexistent pecan orchard in West Texas, he purchased a mineral property in Montana, a mine that had been salted with placer gold. Major Lange learned the hard way that a "producing mine" was often a hole in the ground owned by a confidence man.

Tyler Johnson was a gent of a different stripe than the mineral and lumber speculators Lange had encountered via correspondence. Ty was honest. He did not lie to the men who rode for him, and he did not cheat the man with the money.

Owners meddle is axiomatic in cattle country, but Major Lange was the exception to the rule. He stayed away by half a continent while Tyler Johnson ran the outfit. Ty ran it from top to bottom, left to right.

Just as Lange did not tell the ramrod what to do, he did not object to semi-annual reports that resembled chicken scratchings on a sheet of ruled paper ripped from an eleven by fourteen-inch ledger book. Deposits transferred from the First National Bank of Coalton to the Whitmoor Bank & Trust were the numbers that mattered.

Court O'Hara violated a ranch rule when he drew a bottle of whiskey from his war bag and passed it around. Seated on bunks or stretched out with their boots off, the ranch hands were somber in the aftermath of the burial of Bill Connors. They drank with great seriousness.

Ty left the men to conduct a wake in the bunkhouse. With the exception of Christmas and the 4th of July, hard liquor was not allowed on the place. In practice the rule did not apply to "medicinal" rye whiskey. By leaving the bunkhouse on this day, Ty signaled an intentional ignorance of what would transpire there.

"Be ready to ride at sunup, gents," was the ramrod's sole order to the men as he left the bunkhouse. "We've got live-stock to move."

Lubricated by whiskey, the men did not hold a wake, not in the traditional sense of a commemoration of the Old Sod, but they did take full advantage of Ty's absence to drown sorrows and to reminisce. Well remembered, Bill Connors would be missed on the Circle L.

Dean Bowles received the bottle from Court. He took a slug. Wiping a hand across his mouth, he passed the bottle to Clyde Rand on his right. Clyde drank and passed it to Mike Benning. Mike drank and started to pass it to his right—to the night hawk. When Mike hesitated, the kid reached out and snatched the bottle from his hand. He tilted it to his mouth and drank as though guzzling root beer.

Suddenly gasping for breath, he choked and nearly dropped the bottle. With a timely catch by Mike, it was righted without a spill. While Mike passed it on, the kid's eyes were teary as he struggled for air. By the time the bottle came around again, he had managed to breathe and clear his throat, and he grabbed it. When he raised it to his mouth this time, he took one sensible swallow, and then two more before Court demanded he pass it on.

When the well ran dry, most of the Circle L riders were sloshed and looking for a drowning. Corny obliged. He brought a quart of rye whiskey, strictly medicinal, from the cook shack. The cork squeaked when he pulled it out, and Old Overholt was passed around by the men in the bunk-house.

The night hawk took his full share and then some. He was giddy. Everything he saw, said, or thought was comical. Swaying, the kid walked barefoot the length of the bunkhouse and back, arms spread like a soaring bird. Ranch hands looked on as the kid giggled.

"You figure a night hawk can fly?" asked Mike.

"The sooner the better," Clyde grumbled.

Slurring his words, the kid laughed and claimed he could fly if someone would only bring a bunch of feathers.

"Maybe you oughta climb up on the barn roof," Smitty said. "Flap your arms and jump."

The kid turned to him, grinning. "I told you, ol' Smitty."

"Told me what?" he asked.

"I ain't got enough feathers, ol' Smitty."

Smitty eyed him. "Call me that again, and I'll knock your damned head off."

Wracked by giggles over that prospect, the kid staggered to his bunk and flopped down on it. "Ol' Smitty's gonna knock my head off."

The cowhands reflected on Bill Connors's life on the ranch. A man who guarded his privacy, no one knew where he hailed from or who his kin were. None of the ranch hands had ever asked him point-blank, a courtesy in the West.

One Sunday afternoon Bill had ducked into barn shadows upon the approach of a rider trailing a pack mule. Sporting a handlebar mustache, straw hat, khaki duds, and lace-up boots, the man claimed to be seeking work. He did not look like a cowhand. After a meal in the mess hall for him and feed for his animals, he rode out, angling north.

Bill had remained cautious for days afterward, clearly suspecting the rider was a lawman or bounty hunter. Remote ranches like the Circle L offered refuge to men on the dodge. From that day on the cowhands figured Bill's back trail included a crime committed somewhere, sometime in his past.

Now the hands related anecdotes. Clyde Rand recounted a cold morning when Bill had shaken a dead rattlesnake out of his boot. This had taken place last year in the camp at Ty's Bluff. Not a man noted for washing his socks, the ranch hands had figured the stench from Bill's foot had killed the poor critter.

Court recalled an act of bravery in Coalton last year after roundup. Bill had rushed into the street to free a horse tangled in its harness. Squealing and rearing in a mad effort to kick out of the traces, Bill had eared him down, single-handed, before the animal was injured or the buggy damaged. The horse and rig belonged to Bertha. She had given Bill a free meal and slab of apple pie as a reward.

The kid sat up, bleary-eyed and scowling. "Hell, I never thought much of him."

Silence fell over the men in the bunkhouse with the quiet, deadly weight of a snowslide. A few stole a glance at Smitty before bowing their heads to study the wood grain in the floor.

"What did you say?" Smitty asked.

When the kid did not answer, Mike Benning offered a piece of advice. "Head for the barn, night hawk. This here bunkhouse, it ain't no place for you right now."

"Hell, I'm just telling the truth," the kid retorted. When no one spoke, he dug the hole deeper. "Bill cussed me. He cussed me after I went into the corral to tame that wild mare. You heard him. I damn' near got killed, and Connors, he said I didn't know shit about horses."

"We all heard what Bill said," Dean Bowles answered. "We never have heard your answer."

The kid blinked. "Huh?"

"Just what do you know about horses?" Clyde asked.

"The north end from the south end?" Smitty ventured.

Still slurring his speech, the kid said: "You're just like him."

Smitty stared at him.

"Bill had no call to talk to me like that," the kid went on. "He was mean. That's what I'm saying. Mean as a goddamned snake."

Smitty drew a breath. "Still not answering the question, are you?"

"You can ride a fast horse to hell, ol' Smitty," the kid said to him. He faced the others, his gaze darting from one cowhand to another. "Ever' damned one of you."

Smitty stood. He did not speak. He pointed to the door.

The kid looked at him in surprise.

"Hit it," Smitty ordered.

"Huh?"

"I said, hit it."

With his eyes fixed on Smitty, the kid backtracked. He took one step back and then another, slowly, as though he was about to kick over a beehive and fearing he already had. Dean Bowles moved to his left. Clyde Rand covered the other side. With no avenue of escape, the kid turned and stepped through the doorway, bumping against the door frame as he made his way outside.

The kid halted in the yard. He turned to face his adversary in time to meet a fist. Smitty punched him in the chest, hard. Mouth gaping, the kid staggered. He reached to his waist and grabbed the bone handle of his Green River knife. Drawing the weapon, he went into a crouch, blade up and mouth open as he faced Smitty.

Cowhands crowded into the doorway and pushed their way outside. Smitty slowly advanced, closing the distance.

Ignoring the weapon, he drew back his fist. When he set his feet and feigned a punch, the kid jabbed the knife blade at him in an awkward thrust. The blade cut nothing but air. The next punch was real, a blow to the kid's chin that snapped his head back. The knife fell into the dirt, and the kid went down like a sack of feed.

Smitty stood over him. He watched the kid roll in the dirt and come up to his knees. He managed to stand, his mouth still hanging open.

"You want more?" Smitty asked.

"Go . . . go to hell . . . ol' Smitty."

Smitty stepped in and threw a stiff punch. This one struck the kid's jaw. He went down again and lay in the dirt, gasping. When he managed to roll over and come up on all fours, he lurched, coughed, and suddenly vomited. His head hanging as he gagged, the whiskey and everything else in his stomach dribbled out of his mouth in a shiny, discolored mass. His shoulders quaked when dry heaves wracked him.

"That's enough!"

The door to the ranch house swung open. Boots sounded on the plank porch like a rapid drumbeat. The ranch hands turned to see Ty. Neck bowed, the ramrod descended the steps and crossed the yard in long strides.

"That's enough!" he repeated.

Smitty backed away, fists still clenched. When Ty reached them, he stepped over the vomit, bent down, and helped the kid to his feet.

Ty's gaze swung past Smitty to the men bunched outside the doorway. He demanded to know what had prompted the fight. Smitty told him, and the kid sputtered. Still choking, the kid spat and demanded Ty fire Smitty for fighting.

"I run this outfit," Ty said. He jerked his thumb toward the horse barn. "Get your sougan, kid. You'll sleep in the haymow until I tell you otherwise."

"But Smitty. . . ."

"Go on," Ty said.

"Damn it!" the kid exclaimed. "Smitty busted your stupid rule! What's gonna happen to him?"

Ty faced him. "Son, first thing to remember is, do what you're told. Second thing is, count yourself lucky if you ever amount to half the man Bill was and Smitty is. Go on, now. Get moving."

When the kid made his way to the barn with bedding under his arm, Ty ordered the ranch hands into the bunkhouse. He followed them in and closed the door. After questioning several men, he ripped into all of them.

"What's wrong with you?" he demanded. "Grown men getting a kid liquored up like that. You get him drunk, and then you beat him up. Damn. What's wrong with you?"

After a silence Mike answered: "It was the kid's doing, Ty."

Ty wheeled to face him. "What do you mean by that?"

"He grabbed the bottle and drank it like sarsaparilla," he replied.

"I don't doubt that," Ty said. "After the first drink you should have kept it from him." His gaze swept over them, pausing on Smitty. "You all know it, too. Don't you?"

Head bowed, Smitty did not reply.

"Reckon we had too much to drink," Clyde allowed. "What with Bill, and all."

Dean Bowles was unapologetic. "The kid asked for what he got, Ty. You should 'a' heard him downgrading Bill. Smitty banged on him a little, and the kid puked his guts out." He added: "He'll live."

Court O'Hara said: "Maybe Smitty knocked a wee bit of sense into his noggin."

Ty dismissed their words with a shake of his head. "He's a kid, green as grass. You all know that."

"Well, he's sure-fire old enough to run his damned mouth," Dean countered.

Mike Benning nodded in agreement. "If he's gonna run his mouth thataway, Ty, he's gotta take what comes."

"He pulled his knife on Smitty, too," Dean added. "Tried to carve him up."

Ty paused, taken aback by the depth of their hostility. "You men want me to haul the night hawk back to Coalton and cut him loose? Is that what you're angling for?"

None of them answered until Smitty spoke up. "What do you want us to do, Ty?"

"Leave him alone," the ramrod replied. "Just leave him alone. I'll handle him. If he doesn't measure up, I'll cut him loose. You can bet your bottom dollar on that. Understand?"

Chapter Four

A chill cut the air when Ty stepped out of the ranch house at dawn. With a mug of steaming coffee in hand, he moved to the edge of the verandah. The horizon to the east was aglow. He leaned against a vertical support post while he sipped the brew and admired the view.

His gaze drawn skyward, he looked up. Half a moon, white as snow, was high in the sky. No matter what the almanac said or the calendar read, winter was on the way. He felt it and he smelled it.

In a surge of memories, Ty reflected on that. The sights, sounds, and scents of ranch life brought comfort to him. This sense of familiarity harkened back to his teen years when he had hooked on with the Bar 10, a cattle ranch in central Wyoming. The ranch had represented a safe haven for man and beast. With the livestock tended and stove fires banked, all was right with his corner of the world.

Now Ty's gaze swung to the low-roofed mess hall and cook shack. Wood smoke drifted out of the black stovepipe. Corny had breakfast ready—the usual fare of biscuits and greasy gravy, scrambled eggs, and bacon with the hell fried out of it.

Ty wondered how many riders suffered from whiskey

headaches and deep regrets this morning. A rough day loomed ahead for the men who had overindulged. It was a fine misery to sit a horse when the rider suffered from a throbbing, searing headache. Every angle of sunlight was too bright, all sounds were jarring, each stride painful.

When a horse whinnied, Ty turned toward the barn and adjacent corral. He stiffened. The sight before him amazed him. He saw the kid sitting on the ground near the corral where saddle mounts milled. Head down and knees up, the kid cradled his face in his hands while a lanky cowhand hazed horses from the pasture. That cowhand was Smitty.

Ty spilled coffee in his haste to set the mug down. Descending the verandah steps, he rushed across the yard to the corral. He was baffled by the sight of the kid sitting there, hands covering his face as though sobbing from pain and misery. His temper flared with every step. Had Smitty beaten the kid again? Ty could not believe the top hand would disobey him, yet how else could this sight be explained?

Smitty hazed the last three saddle mounts into the corral and closed the gate. When Ty approached, the kid raised his head and looked up at him. Ty saw a bruised face.

"What's going on here?" Ty demanded.

Smitty stepped closer, grinning sheepishly as he leaned against the smooth top rail. "I know you want the night hawk to work his own chores, Ty, but this time I figured I'd lend a hand. He's not feeling too rosy. Hardly ate a bite at breakfast, what with the liquor still hammering him."

"You . . . ?" Ty paused as he absorbed the meaning of the scene before him. "You are . . . helping him?"

"Yeah," Smitty said. He pulled his hat off and ran a hand through thinning hair. "You were right, Ty."

"About what?"

"What I done yesterday," Smitty said. "It was wrong. Plumb wrong. The liquor wrung good sense out of my brain. That's the only thing I can figure. I told the kid I was sorry for it. I aim to give him a hand today. Even up the score a little, maybe."

Relieved Smitty had not handed the kid another beating, Ty was equally glad he had not jumped the gun by accusing his top hand of wrongdoing.

"We'll be ready to ride when you are, Ty," Smitty went on. "The kid here, he'll give Corny a hand with the chuck wagon. Said he'd tend to the sale horses as our night hawk, too."

"Is that so?" Ty asked him.

The kid nodded.

"Speak up," Smitty urged him.

"Reckon so," the kid mumbled, avoiding the ramrod's gaze.

Smitty turned to him. "Ty, what do you think of letting the night hawk ride that roan on the drive? It's a purty good horse. And there's a saddle in the barn nobody's using."

Ty nodded slowly, playing dumb. He had no doubt the kid put Smitty up to this request, no doubt that it was another way to make things right after handing him a beating.

"I'll help him out if he needs it," Smitty added.

Ty answered with deliberation or something like it. "Reckon we could use another rider on the trail drive."

The kid managed half a smile as he stole a glance at the ramrod.

"Drink plenty of water today, kid," Smitty went on, "and you'll work off that headache. Remember the pain next time someone offers you whiskey for anything besides a snakebite. Take it from me. I have more experience with the morning after a long night than I like to admit. Don't you repeat my mistakes. Hear?"

The kid acknowledged his advice with a single nod.

"Go give Corny a hand," Ty said to him.

Elbowed by Smitty, the kid answered: "Yes, Mister Johnson."

Ty covered a smile as he turned and headed back to the ranch house. A new thought came to him. As rebellious and sullen as the kid was, maybe Smitty would be the one to tame him.

The annual cattle drive from Circle L headquarters to the Coalton pens was always an exercise in frustration, at times a dangerous one. This year all but two ranch hands would make the ride. Dean Bowles and George Taylor had volunteered to stay on the ranch to look after critters and keep up with the chores. Ty would bring their pay upon his return from town.

This arrangement was requested by the two ranch hands. Last year, after roundup, they had lost a month's wages during one bleary night. Awakening in a back alley, skunk drunk, they discovered their pockets turned inside out, their feet bare. This year, neither man would lose his boots or hard-earned dollars to rigged gaming tables, to marked cards, or to the beckoning smile of a dance-hall chippie.

From the ranch to Coalton was a two- or three-day ride, depending on the horse. Herding steers along the same route, drovers faced six or seven days of eating dust by day and sleeping in their sougans on hard ground by night—and possibly a drive longer than that, depending on weather and the pace maintained by the steers.

There was no easy way to do it. The distance from here to there was too short to identify and bell a leader, and not long enough to whip ornery steers into a trail-broke herd.

"Push them," Ty instructed Circle L riders new to this drive. "Head the bastards out, and push them. Somehow or another, we'll all get to Coalton right-side up."

In unfamiliar terrain the steers spooked easily. Ungainly as they looked, range-wise cattle were agile and quick to run. A creature as harmless as a butterfly taking wing or something as insignificant as the flash of sunlight off a belt buckle could start a run. Three years ago a swirling gust of wind caught the paper wrapper from a sack of Arbuckles coffee. It set off a stampede. In that one, five market-ready steers had been injured and two men trampled when thrown.

All day, every day of the drive, steers had to be herded over low hills and in and out of ravines. Ranch hands coaxed them with shrill whistling and pushed them with shouted threats. The commands were backed up by the *whack* of a whip handle or the sting of a willow switch across a broad back.

When Ty and Smitty brought out the body of Bill Connors, they had not tarried. They made no effort to locate and gather the steers the two ranch hands had rousted out of thickets bordering a wetland. That was a job for another day.

On the Coalton drive now, the drovers had their hands full. Bonehead critters kept circling back. Bawling, they were soon followed by other bunch quitters. From time to time the herd that had been moving along pretty as you please suddenly wheeled. Lead steers angled north in their determination to return to familiar pastures and known water holes—not unlike two-legged critters rushing toward their favorite saloon after a long ride.

For man and beast in the West, a reliable source of water

marked the margin between success and failure, between life and death. If wells went dry, a town site was abandoned. Buildings were picked clean of usable lumber, doors, casement windows, hinges, and all manner of hardware. Skeleton-like remains of buildings were left, windswept and weathered, slowly yielding to the forces of nature.

Coalton was founded near mineral springs. The town benefited from an endless supply of water, at once cursed by sulphuric odors. Hot at its source, the springs took on turquoise-green hues where it pooled underground—how deep, how hot, or how many gurgling springs fed the pools, no one knew.

Gruesome stories abounded. Tales of hapless wanderers, merrily drunk and singing off-key to the stars, recounted the fate of men who had stumbled into a roiling pool. Those storied victims of one misstep flailed and screamed while cooked alive.

"Well, at least that damned caterwauling stopped," locals were reputed to have said when the struggle ended. Apocryphal or not, mothers threatened their children with a whaling if they so much as ventured close to those steaming springs.

Thick with algae and trailing long, mossy tendrils, the water exuded a faint odor of sulphur in summer. In winter the thermal springs were marked by steam rising from the surface in wispy clouds. Some residents believed the spring water to be an elixir. They drank it for health reasons. Others boiled it for health reasons.

Long before the town's founding, travelers in wagon caravans called this place Stink Water Junction. Odorous or not, surging spring waters were welcomed in those days, and later proved to be the key to Coalton's prosperity. The local economy was secured by irrigated farms nearby, by far-flung ranches with stock ponds, by the water tower of the Union Pacific Railroad spur, and by mule-drawn water tankers in daily runs to the Black Diamond coal mine. Taken from any angle, water was the lifeblood of the town.

Coalton was anchored at one end of Front Street by a church with a steeple, the other by a school with a bell tower. Radiating out from the business district, graded streets and avenues with plank walkways led to residences behind picket fences.

On the other side of the railroad tracks, 100 yards beyond the U.P. water tower, cribs and crude cabins sported lamps with red chimneys. Scattered among them, saloons, gambling dens, and dance halls prospered, as though these deadfalls had sprung up downwind from the municipality. The two entities co-existed, more or less, with Sheriff Rogers and two deputies maintaining standards of acceptable behavior in both.

Each establishment had its own clientele. Like the Comet, some saloons favored townsfolk and ranch hands, and disallowed drunkenness. Others favored Italian miners, or loggers and sawyers, or railroad crews and section gangs. Not that a paying customer was ever turned away for not belonging to the right bunch, but, like cattle in a herd, men tended to congregate in familiar groups and in time had come to prefer certain establishments over others.

On the fifth day out, Ty spurred his mount and rode ahead of the plodding herd. His plan was to arrive in Coalton a day or two before his drovers reached the pens.

He succeeded. Boarding his horse in Jim's livery, he strode past Clancy's bookstore, Bob Meyer's gunsmith shop, and the sheriff's office on his way to the Union Pacific cage in the depot. He confirmed cattle cars reserved for the

Circle L were *en route*. Via telegraph, he accepted the going price of beef at the Chicago slaughterhouses. With the remaining task of pushing the steers through slanted chutes into cattle cars, he knew the next day or two would be hectic.

Angling across Front Street past the tie rail at the Coalton House, Ty drew a deep breath. The odor was unique to this town. Unlike the pervasive scents of animals and feed and stock ponds on the ranch, the air in town reeked of coal fumes. Smoke from the chimneys of business buildings and the stovepipes of household cook stoves combined in a distinct odor with the rotten-egg scent from the hot springs.

Ty waited for a coach to pass, and stepped off the boardwalk. He crossed the street toward the bank, waving through the window at the bank president, Arthur Blaine. The banker met him at the door.

"That time of year, eh?" Blaine said, holding his hand out.

Ty shook his hand. "So the calendar tells me."

"Every year goes by faster than the last one," he observed.

Ty followed him through the bank to a black, steel-plated vault with dual combination locks. A painted gold frame decorated the door with a landscape painting portraying snow-capped mountain peaks and a blue sky over pine trees and a rushing creek. Across the bottom the manufacturer's name was printed in elaborate script: Dual Lock.

Blaine pulled the vault door open. As usual he wore a pin-striped vest with a silver watch chain, sleeve garters on each arm, and a green visor over his eyes. With his white shirt and starched collar, Ty often wondered how the man kept so clean and sharply creased. While Ty would not trade with any man, the life of a desk jockey held a certain appeal—even though a painting of a mountain scene hardly measured up to the real thing in the Cheyenne Mountains.

Ty drew out enough cash to settle up at the mercantile and to cover a month's pay for each ranch hand, with a bonus. His wallet thus fattened and coin sack weighted, he left the bank and crossed the street again.

Bertha's Home Cooking Café was flanked by Anne Marie's Millinery on one side and the Coalton Mercantile on the other. That two-story frame building housed an Odd Fellows hall upstairs. One corner of the bay window up there displayed a **Doctor** sign. The shingle for the county land agent hung in the opposite corner window.

Ty knocked trail dust from his hat as he entered the café. A clatter of pans and the commotion of splashing water came from the kitchen. With few diners in Bertha's eatery at mid-afternoon, ringing spur rowels caught her attention. She came out of the kitchen, wet hands on her hips. A stout woman with graying hair, the web of wrinkles in her brow deepened in a frown.

"Howdy, Bertha," Ty said.

She gestured to a window. Framed by lace curtains, the panes faced the tonsorial parlor across the street. "Tyler, there's a rumor going around town."

"What's that?"

"Rumor says you will find a tub of hot, soapy water in the back room of the tonsorial parlor," she said. "A pail of cologne is in there, too, I hear."

Unconcerned, Ty made his way to the table by the window looking out on Front. He pulled a chair out and sat down.

"Why?" he asked her. "You in need of a soak?"

"One of us sure is," she replied, turning up her nose.

"Reckon this is Stink Water Junction," Ty said.

"It's not the water, Tyler," she said. "It's the cowboys."

"I won't stay long enough to drive off the customers you haven't poisoned yet."

"That's a comfort," she said.

"I was just down at the depot," he went on. "Westbound's due in a couple hours."

She nodded slowly, undoubtedly having memorized train schedules a long time ago. "What of it?"

"Figured I'd eat early," Ty explained, "so I won't be hogging a table while you're slopping train passengers and townsfolk. By then, I'll be in the Coalton House, soaking in a tub at the end of the hall."

Bertha's frown turned to a smile. "Son-of-a-bitch stew, cowboy? With a slab of apple pie and a dollop of whipped cream?"

Ty entered the Coalton House through doors with etched glass panels. As the doors swung shut, he caught a glimpse of himself. He saw a craggy face and the reflected image of a cowhand in Western garb from battered riding boots to a sweat-rimmed stockman's hat.

Crossing the lobby with saddlebags slung over his shoulder, he checked in at the desk. The clerk greeted him with a hearty—"Good day, Mister Johnson!"—and handed him the key to 201, the second-floor suite overlooking Front that he favored every year after roundup.

Ty mounted the staircase. The pleasures of sleeping in a real bed, eating in the hotel restaurant, smoking a Havana, and leaving his boots and hat in the hall to be polished and brushed by morning were luxuries he granted himself once a year. At other times of the year he was frugal. When he drove the buckboard on supply runs to Coalton, he saved money by sleeping in a rooming house near the tracks. The days after roundup were unique. Shipping cattle was a mighty goal achieved, a time for celebration, a time to live it up before winter hit.

In the suite, Ty opened a saddlebag and took out his ivory-handled straight razor. Shaving soap with a cup and a brush, a strop, and towels were provided in bathing rooms located at either end of the hall. Ty went to the nearest one to shave and bathe. Hot water piped in from thermal springs afforded a steaming bath for as long as a man could take it.

Later, with shades pulled and curtains drawn in the suite, he stretched out on the bed. He heard a train come and go. Hoof beats and clinking harness chains drifted to him from the street. Staring into darkness, random thoughts drifted through his mind. He reflected on occurrences in the past year, events ranging from hiring a footloose kid to the death of Bill Connors. Like a pebble tossed into still water, such happenstances rippled through the lives of the men on the Circle L.

The hotel suite was so dark and so quiet that he dozed through the evening and slept all night without stirring. At mid-morning, shamefully late, he descended the flight of carpeted stairs for breakfast in the restaurant. Late or not, he lingered over coffee and a pastry there while perusing a copy of the Laramie *Boomerang*. The newspaper was hot off the press only three days ago, a benefit of regular train service.

Ty went to the livery. After exchanging pleasantries with Jim, he saddled his horse and rode out of town. He did not mention the ponies to the liveryman. That would come later. He followed a course roughly paralleling the railroad

64

tracks and the line of creosote-coated poles supporting telegraph wires. Long-eared jack rabbits bounded away from
him, locusts leaped, and coveys of sparrows took wing.

He reined up and peered ahead. The herd would come
this way. He dismounted and took makings out of his vest
pocket. Shaking tobacco onto the paper, he rolled a cigarette
and sealed it with the tip of his tongue. Firing it with a friction match, he smoked until he spotted a brown haze on the
horizon. Before long the sounds of bawling steers reached his
ears. He ground out the cigarette under his boot. Striding to
his horse, he grasped the horn, thrust the toe of his boot into
the stirrup, and swung up in one fluid motion.

Presently Ty saw drovers, grimy men eating a steady diet
of dust stirred by Circle L livestock. When they spotted Ty,
they greeted him with catcalls and whistling. Such joshing
and hoo-rawing were reserved for a cowhand caught in an
advanced state of cleanliness, hair combed, too. With the
pretext of concealing their identities behind bandannas
now, the riders were emboldened to treat the ramrod as just
another hired hand.

"My, but don't he look spanking clean!"

"Shiny as a new dollar, ain't he?"

"Naw, the ramrod's cheap as a steel penny."

"Wish I could get me a hot, soapy bath somewheres!"

"Did your ma scrub you down this morning, sonny?"

Ty grinned as he gave the herd a wide berth. "Keep
these critters moving, gents, keep 'em moving."

The kid brought up the rear. With a dust-caked bandanna tied snugly over his mouth and nose like the ranch
hands, the youngster rode drag. His job was to herd sale
horses and pick up stragglers. Farther back, Corny drove
the chuck wagon at a slow pace.

Ty neck-reined his horse around, and from there he led

the way to the Coalton siding.

With four-legged critters safe in holding pens and all accounted for on Ty's tally, the men made a beeline for the Comet. Elbow to elbow at the long bar in there, they downed mugs of beer to wet their whistles—until a train whistle sounded.

The mournful call drifted across the prairie as a locomotive pulled a long line of mixed freight and cattle cars. Like some great, hissing beast, it rolled past the platform and steep-roofed Coalton station. Slowing, the engine eased toward the chutes and stopped beyond them.

The men of the Circle L downed foaming beer and bolted from the saloon. Untying their horses at the rail outside, they swung up and rode hell for leather back to the pens. On a slow horse, the kid brought up the rear. In the saloon, he had been allowed to stand at the bar with Circle L hands as long as he confined his consumption of liquid refreshment to root beer.

Ty noticed the kid had put on some weight since that afternoon when they had first met in the Comet. No longer a scarecrow, he had gained some muscle through his upper chest and shoulders. And now he was tolerated, Ty noted, while working alongside the men.

Children gathered to watch. Ty glimpsed the kid squaring his shoulders as he made an attempt to sit tall in a Western saddle cinched to the sway-backed roan. Head turning, the kid watched his shadow cast by the afternoon sun. If he did not cut a dashing figure on horseback for the benefit of his young audience, it was not for a lack of trying. With the bandanna pulled over his beardless jaw, the kid looked the part. He could just about pass for a seasoned cowhand with his sweat-stained, dusty garb and a wide-brimmed hat.

To his credit, the kid had helped Corny with chuck wagon chores all the way from the ranch. He wrangled sale horses and went after bunch quitters on that slow horse—all of this work without a curse or complaint. Ty learned from Corny that Smitty had lent a hand now and then, and, between them, the work was done day and night with no steers or ponies lost on the drive.

Ty hollered to get the kid's attention. Answering the shout with a sweeping wave of his hat, the kid made a great show of helping the ramrod haze the horses down Front Street and into the corral at Jim's livery. The liveryman stepped out of the barn. Eyes narrowing, he shoved his straw hat up on his forehead.

"Damned broomtails," he muttered.

"Reckon there's some good stock among them," Ty allowed.

Jim shook his head. "Good for glue, maybe."

Ty did not take the derisive remarks personally. Such banter was part of the negotiating process, and a horse trader could not be faulted for trying to set a low price at the outset. They both knew at some point a deal would be struck, usually after one of them slapped his hat across his leg and stomped away in utter disgust, one accusing the other of outright thievery, one reminding the other that he had children to feed. After the deal was done and money paid, both men would resume their easy-going friendship.

The liveryman requested more time to observe the "prairie nags" before making a bid. Ty agreed to that stipulation. He left the ponies milling in the corral and rode away with the kid following on the roan.

On the way back to the U.P. pens at the far end of Front Street, the door to the sheriff's office swung open. Sheriff Rogers stepped out. He lifted his hand to flag down Ty.

"Howdy, Wade," Ty said, drawing rein.

Dapper as ever in a gray suit, Rogers halted at the edge of the plank walk. He acknowledged the kid's presence, and turned his attention to the ramrod.

"I know you're busy right now, Ty," Rogers said. "Let's get together when you have more time. If I don't see you before you leave town, stop by my office."

Ty replied with a nod. He detected a cryptic tone in the lawman's voice, and wondered what was on his mind. At once he sensed a private matter at hand and knew this was not the time or place to ask.

Rogers turned his attention to the kid. "How's ranch life treating you?"

"Good enough," he mumbled.

"They feeding you out there?" he asked.

"Yeah."

"You must be taking to it," Rogers said.

"Reckon so," the kid muttered.

With a last look at Ty, Rogers stepped back from the edge of the boardwalk. He touched fingertips to his hat brim in parting, and returned to his office.

By evening, the last of the Circle L steers had been loaded, sixteen to a car. With thumps and a loud banging of couplings, the engine hissed and huffed. It inched away, and slowly built speed with black coal smoke billowing from the stack.

Ty saw Smitty beckon to the kid. Walking stride for stride, the two of them headed for the tonsorial parlor. With Smitty watching over him, Ty figured the kid faced a scrubbing before an evening of drinking root beer and a night sleeping in a rooming house.

The next morning Corny and the ranch hands filed into

Ty's suite in the Coalton House. Joined by Smitty and the kid, this was their last pay day of the season. Ty noted both the night hawk and Smitty were clean and sober this morning, and figured he had guessed correctly about Smitty's influence on the kid.

Ty was not one to stake out the high ground for a round of speechifying, but, with the men gathered around him in the suite, he took this opportunity to thank them for their service and loyalty. These men had risked their necks in the everyday course of their labors, and now Ty expressed his gratitude to them.

Among them, respect for the ramrod ran high, and parting company ignited an emotionally charged moment. Ty bowed his head. He presided over a period of silence to honor the memory of Bill Connors. His whispered eulogy cut deeply, ending with "So long, ol' hoss."

Stone-faced until then, Smitty's chin quivered. He sniffled, and wiped his bandanna over his face to cover his weeping. The other men looked away or studied the floor, but the kid watched him.

Ty invited the riders to come back to the Circle L, encouraging them to sign on next spring. He figured some would rejoin him on the ranch. Others would not. He had never managed to keep a full crew intact. Now, each man filed past him for a last handshake and a month's pay, plus one gold eagle as a bonus for roundup duties.

Ty was aware Smitty and the kid held back. They paused in the hallway, hanging back outside the door to the suite.

Ty gave instructions to Corny. He told the ranch cook to restock the chuck wagon at the mercantile and to purchase supplies as needed, with one quart of rye whiskey included on the Circle L account. They would pull out tomorrow, he said, and head back to the home ranch.

When Corny left, Ty turned his attention to Smitty and the kid in the hallway. He saw them glance at one another, clearly teetering on the precipice of a question to the ramrod, an important one.

Ty recalled anger flaring into violence in the drunken aftermath of Bill Connors's burial. The one-sided fight between Smitty and the kid had had a long-range effect, one the ramrod did not expect and would never have believed possible if he had not seen it for himself. For the kid filled a void. In a sense, he had taken Bill Connors's place in Smitty's life.

Ty gave this pairing some thought. He wondered if he was reading their expressions right, and beckoned to them. "Smitty," he said, "you and the night hawk. Come here."

When they stepped into the suite, Ty said: "We need to palaver."

With the two of them standing before him, Ty offered to hire them for a season's work. "Would you gents be interested in staying on the Circle L through the winter?"

Depending on weather conditions, ranch work in winter was generally not as strenuous or as risky as the tasks of rounding up cattle, roping, throwing, and branding yearlings in the spring. Winter duty was monotonous, a matter of hunkering down while blizzards roared and temperatures plummeted. A ranch hand could accumulate money in winter because, short of bucking snowdrifts on a long, cold ride to Coalton, he had no place to spend his pay.

As he thought about it, though, Ty expected them to decline his offer. For one thing, the kid disliked him. Ty had no illusions about his ill will. Second, the kid was eager to shed endless chores, and now he had some money in his pocket and rudimentary skills under his belt. He could leave Coalton as a paying passenger in a train car or board a stagecoach for parts unknown. Either way, he would be free of barked orders from the ramrod, free to call his own shots without fear of starvation or a whipping. He just might hook on with another cattle ranch down the line.

In addition, Ty knew Smitty had relatives in New Mexico Territory. If he and the kid partnered up, Ty figured they would head south for the winter like migratory critters tracking the warmth of the sun. He was, therefore, more than a little surprised by Smitty's reply.

"Last night, me and the kid, we talked it over. Just like you said, Ty, when snow hits, there ain't much to do on a ranch but stay alive, bust ice in stock ponds, and sled hay to the critters. A man can save up a pot full of money after the snow flies."

Ty turned to the kid. "Is that your thinking, too?"

He nodded. "I aim to buy me a horse and saddle, come spring."

Smitty grinned and extended his hand to the ramrod. "Reckon we'll stick, Ty . . . me and this here night hawk, if you can tolerate us."

Ty shook Smitty's hand and then shook the kid's outstretched hand when he held it out like a dead fish. He figured the kid had taken advice from Smitty, accepting words of wisdom that would have gone unheeded had they come from anyone else. No matter the source, Ty figured the kid was using his head for a change.

Chapter Five

Blasts from a train whistle, the ringing of the engine's brass bell, and the clanging of car couplings were sounds common to Coalton. But when a train arrived at 3:00 a.m., Ty was awakened, roused by a commotion outside.

He left the bed. Pulling a curtain aside, he lifted the shade and looked out the window. He saw railroad men throwing switches and swinging lanterns. Among the dancing shadows, voices carried to him as trainmen shouted instructions to one another. The conductor directed an engine with four Pullman coaches to the far siding where half a dozen freight cars, rolling stock empty and out of service, awaited repairs.

Returning to bed, Ty slept fitfully. He dreamt of a phantom train. A locomotive pulled a long line of cattle cars. Circle L steers were somehow turned loose—all of them. A mad chase led back to the home ranch. In the disconnected logic of a nightmare Ty found the livestock grazing contentedly there. A man alone, he had no hope of driving them back to the Coalton pens. . . .

In the wakeful aftermath of that dream of failure, details were still fresh in his mind when he went downstairs for breakfast. It was only a dream, yet he felt troubled by the images lingering in his mind. In the restaurant he overheard diners at another table talking about four private cars that had rolled in late last night and now stood on a siding, window shades lowered.

As Ty lifted a white porcelain coffee cup to his mouth, he heard his name spoken in the lobby. The hotel desk was positioned around the corner from an arched entryway to the restaurant, out of his line of vision. Ty heard the disembodied voice of the clerk answer a query from someone out there.

"Yes, sir. You'll find Mister Tyler Johnson taking his breakfast in the restaurant. He's seated at the first table on your right. That way. Yes, sir. You're welcome, sir."

Ty figured it was one of the cowhands, and he turned to see which one had come looking for him. Instead of a ranch hand, a stranger entered the restaurant from the lobby. The well-dressed man sported a Vandyke beard. Short and slight of build, his eyes darted left and right before his gaze came to rest on the ramrod. He approached the table with his felt hat in hand.

"Tyler Johnson? Mister Tyler Johnson?"

Ty nodded in mute reply. He lowered his coffee cup, eyeing this dandy. He wore a tailored brown suit with a satin vest showcasing a gold chain and fob.

"My mother died," he said.

Appearances can be deceiving. So can adages, Ty thought as he looked at the gentleman standing before him. Neither wild-eyed nor foaming at the mouth, the man looked respectable. Yet by any rational measure, Ty reckoned he was in the presence of a well-dressed gent gone mad.

"Sir?"

"My mother died," he repeated. He tugged at his pointed beard, a mannerism that made him appear all the

73

more gnome-like. "You may not know it yet, Mister Johnson, but that fact holds meaning for you as well as for me. Her passing is the reason I am here, the reason I traveled by rail halfway across this great continent."

Ty stared at him.

"I am here to tour my ranch," the gentleman continued, "and to view livestock bearing my brand."

My ranch . . . my brand . . . ? Ty felt powerless to do anything but stare. The aftermath of a dream of lost cattle somehow threaded its way into this bizarre encounter with a city dude gone mad.

"Oh, I should explain, shouldn't I?" he said suddenly. "My apologies if I am confusing you. I shall explain, post haste." He gestured to a chair at the table. "May I join you?" He did not wait for an answer.

Ty warily watched him pull the chair out. Breakfast with a lunatic would be a new experience.

"My mother," he said as he sat down, "was Margaret Payson Lange."

Even then Ty did not fit the puzzle pieces together into a recognizable picture. The terms "my ranch" and "my brand" still made no sense to him. In dream fragments, he kept thinking about lost cattle. Dream or no dream, he had never heard of a woman by the name of Margaret Payson. As one awkward moment dragged into another, the surname rattled through his mind. He repeated it aloud—twice. "Lange. Lange." Of course the name was familiar, but, like an echo from the past, he found no connection to reality in it.

"You know me by our infrequent correspondence and my signature scrawled on various documents over the years," the man said. He drew a breath and smiled. "Mister Johnson, I must say I am pleased to make your acquaintance in person, very pleased, indeed . . . face to face, eye to eye."

Ty watched him. The gent paused, waiting, as though the matter was settled. Ty was not a man to stammer, but at that moment he was unable to utter a reasoned reply. "Are you . . . uh . . . are you . . . uh . . . ?" His voice trailed off. He blurted out his question. "Who the hell are you?"

"Lange," the gent stated, as if everyone walking the earth knew him. "Major Gregory Lange, sir, of Whitmoor, Maryland."

Inwardly reeling from the shock of this odd introduction, Ty attempted to gather his thoughts. "Mister Lange, uh . . . we, uh . . . we shipped yesterday."

"Shipped?"

Ty nodded. "Circle L cattle were shipped by rail yesterday. I sent the money to your Maryland bank by telegraph."

"Yes, yes, I am sure you did," Major Lange said. "You are always punctual. The bank transfer must have come after I left Whitmoor."

Ty thought about that. The mere fact that he sat across the table from the owner of the Circle L still stunned him. *This little man is Major Lange?* For some unknown reason Ty had expected him to be bigger, more forceful. Why, he did not know. Given his preference for staying back East in Maryland, Ty had never considered the possibility of actually meeting the man. Now he tried to think of something to say, anything coherent to say to him. "Reckon those beeves are bawling in the Chicago stockyards by now. You must have passed a long line of eastbound cattle cars on your way here."

Major Lange nodded slowly. "Why yes, now that you mention it, we were relegated to a siding while the conductor yielded to an oncoming train. I remember seeing slatted boxcars pass us by. And now you are informing me Circle L livestock were in those cars?"

"Yes, sir," Ty said, "I reckon I am."

The irony of this miscue did not escape Major Lange. "Out there on that great plain, we staged a croquet match. We were whacking colored balls around clumps of weeds when that train roared by us."

"If I had been notified," Ty said, "I would have held the steers here another day for your inspection."

"Is there a telegraph wire to the ranch headquarters?" he asked.

Ty shook his head. "No."

"That's what I thought," Major Lange said. "Had I sent a letter via Coalton, general delivery, you would not have seen it for weeks, would you?"

Ty acknowledged that point. "Reckon not."

"Just as I thought," Major Lange said. "Allow me to explain. My mother was in failing health for a long while, and, when she passed away, I made arrangements for my Western trip. I left Whitmoor almost immediately after the funeral." Major Lange drew a breath and continued: "From Maryland to Colorado, I have dealt with more railroad lines than you can shake a stick at. Train schedules are as tangled as a bucket of snakes, I assure you. On the way here we idled away hours and hours on sidings while waiting for freight or passenger trains to go through. We passed the time by playing croquet and lawn-bowling in high grass. In the car we played checkers or cards. I do believe we wore out a deck playing hearts."

Ty eyed him, wondering what he meant by "we".

Major Lange went on: "I knew the dates you typically shipped cattle, and I thought we could intercept you and the Circle L range riders."

Lange shook his head ruefully. "Well, what's done is done. Now we wish to tour my ranch and view herds of my cattle and my horses galloping across the wide open spaces of the American West. Shall we depart tomorrow? As you might guess, having outlived my mother, I am keen to get on with life itself."

Ty stared. That was the strangest remark he had ever heard.

After breakfast they made their way down Front and crossed the tracks to the private cars on the far siding. A question still loomed in his mind. Ty wondered if Major Lange was in the habit of using the royal "we", or if he was traveling with guests?

He looked past the diminutive man. Shades were drawn in windows of a Pullman sleeper car, but in the parlor car the shades were up. Ty saw shadows moving about inside.

"Mister Lange . . . ," he began.

"Call me major," he interrupted. "May I address you as Tyler?"

"My friends call me Ty."

"Ty, it is," Major Lange said. "Now . . . you were about to say?"

Ty asked: "You're traveling with guests?"

Major Lange nodded and tugged at his beard. "You will meet my fiancée . . . Miss Rose Durning. We are accompanied by my future sister-in-law, Miss Snapdragon Durning."

With a brief, mischievous smile one might have expected from a gnome, Major Lange elaborated in a tone of mock confidentiality. "Her given name is Sharon, but I call her Snapdragon behind her back. You will soon understand why, just as you will understand the reasons I am betrothed to Rose and not to her. The ladies are eager to meet a real rancher and observe range riders performing their duties with alacrity. Horses galloping across the great plain, cows lassoed for branding . . . all of that adventure is a daily occurrence in the wild West, correct?"

"All of it," Ty allowed.

"First, though, won't you join us for dinner?" Major Lange said. "Edgar and Millicent will prepare your evening meal . . . simple fare, but adequate, I assure you."

"Edgar and Millicent?" Ty repeated.

"My manservant doubles as chef," Lange said, "and his wife serves as maid to the ladies in the privacy of their car. Which reminds me . . . I must give Edgar and Millicent a count. We can seat ten in the dining car." He asked: "How many guests will you bring, Ty?"

The ramrod stared at him. Guests? Except for meals given to drifters he had encountered on Circle L range, Ty had never actually invited anyone to dinner. Stumped by the request, he could only manage a shrug.

"Come now," Major Lange said. "You must know someone around here who can join us."

"My ranch cook, Cornelius, is in town," Ty said. "So is one of my Circle L riders . . . Smitty. The night hawk is here, too. I reckon they can pack in some chow at your table."

"Night hawk?" Major Lange repeated.

"It's a nickname the kid goes by," Ty said.

"Colorful terminology," Lange observed. "A kid, you say?"

"On cattle ranches out here," Ty explained, "the night hawk tends horses, repairs tack, and gets all the chores done after dark."

"Oh, yes, I see," Lange said, clearly acquainting himself with a vocabulary that was new and novel. "The chore boy takes orders from the overseer, day and night, not unlike a plantation, correct?"

"That's about the size of it," Ty said.

"Where I come from," Major Lange said, "the night hawk flies in darkness in search of sustenance. I have read that particular bird is related to the whippoorwill, according to ornithologists."

Ty saw his gaze shift from railroad cars to Front Street.

"Perhaps you can tell me where I may find the chief law officer of this township," Lange said.

"The county sheriff?" Ty asked.

"Oh, yes, of course," he repeated. "County. You are divided into counties out here, not townships."

Ty turned and pointed toward Front. "Sheriff Rogers's office and the jailhouse are on the far end of the street, across from the livery. You'll see a star painted on the window."

"For the illiterate, I presume?"

"Reckon so."

"I shall invite the sheriff to our *soirée,* as well," Major Lange said. The mischievous smile lit his face again. "East or West, county or township, there can be no harm in befriending the man who upholds the law, now can there?"

Ty nodded in mute reply. He was thinking about *"soirée"*. He did not ask, but figured it had something to do with chow.

"Tell me," Major Lange said, "is this sheriff of yours married?"

"His wife's name is Elizabeth."

"Then we shall reserve a setting for Missus Elizabeth Rogers, as well." Major Lange slapped his hands together.

"Eight o'clock this evening, then, my dining car is the appointed place. Agreed?"

Ty had never seen anything like it—not in a train car or a restaurant. Among tureens with porcelain bowls and elegant dinner dishes, a baked trifle was set aside for dessert. The sponge cake was soaked in rum and topped with a custard.

In a sidelong glance Ty could see Corny had never pulled a chair up to such dinner courses, either. The ranch cook gawked. The sheriff and his wife sat across the table from Smitty and the kid, all of them stilled as though they had taken a breath in unison and held it.

In this narrow environment of walnut panels, high-backed upholstered chairs, tasseled drapery, and polished brass lamps, a pâte was served after broth had been ladled into bowls by Millicent. A somber, thick-bodied woman, she served the meal with a practiced efficiency while Edgar worked in the cramped kitchen. Ty glimpsed the man in there, a bull-necked servant as muscular as a plowman.

The whole array of buttered rice, steamed root vegetables, and baked goods etched a scowl in the kid's face. He stared at the pastry shell on his plate while Major Lange described the contents—a thick paste made from goose liver, pork fat, onions, and mushrooms. This unsightly chow was arranged on a white dinner plate with silver service, crystal goblets, and fine linen. Candelabrum ablaze, such opulence had the effect of further silencing the dinner guests seated at the narrow table in the dining car.

After introductions were made by Major Lange, the two sisters stole glances at one another, cocked their heads like birds, and struck thoughtful poses. In truth, they had little in common and even less to talk about with the guests. The diners merely watched as gleaming silver and strange food was set before them by Edgar and Millicent, both servants clad in tailored black and gray uniforms befitting their station back East.

Ty eyed Rose and then sneaked a look at Snapdragon. The two sisters were dissimilar. Large, Rose was decked out in Victorian splendor with pearls draped over flowing fabric as heavy as armor. Her gaze took in the guests before she cast a lingering look with a stiff smile at the diminutive Major Lange.

Ty did not miss the unspoken message from fiancée to fiancé: *We are trapped here, my dear, surrounded by bumpkins.*

Sharon was reedy. Thin as a weed, she wore a simple cotton dress reaching from shoulder to foot, the garment loosely gathered at her waist. Both sisters shared a complaint, namely the pervasive stench in this bleak land. A distinctly sulphuric odor drifted from a spring nearby. Where, they neither knew nor inquired. They insisted on leaving this horrible place at once.

"Aside from the stink," Rose said, "I find the desert to be oppressive. And dusty."

"As do I," Sharon said. "Yes."

"It's barren," Rose said. "The land stretches out with nothing to break the monotony but dust devils. Back home we have trees and flowers in abundance, wonderful, luxuriant vegetation in full leaf."

"This land is empty," Sharon echoed, and added her own contribution to mutual misery: "And dust gets into everything."

"Everything," Rose repeated emphatically, and turned to her future husband. "Don't you agree?"

Instead of answering directly, Major Lange attempted to mollify the women. He promised to show them the storied

Circle L Ranch tomorrow. After all, that was their primary goal, wasn't it? Whether they liked or disliked this terrain was not at issue. Upon their return home to Whitmoor, he reminded them, every doubter would be silenced. The fact of his ownership of a Colorado cattle ranch stretching to distant horizons would be confirmed once and for all.

Ty's jaw was clenched throughout this exchange. He could have told the sisters where the sulphuric smell came from. He could have explained what a reliable source of water meant to the town of Coalton and to the region, but sensed they did not wish to know. The pair merely sought an excuse to leave, he figured.

Ty did not undermine Major Lange's stated plan, either, by informing them a two-day trip by carriage, not one day, awaited them. They would discover that soon enough. By then, turning back would be more painful than continuing on to the ranch. Ty suspected that was Major Lange's scheme—that is, to take on one argument at a time.

"Young man," Rose asked suddenly, eyebrows arching as she turned to the kid, "I have been wondering. Exactly how did you acquire that name? Was it given to you like some accolade?"

Ty saw the kid answer with a self-conscious shrug.

She pressed him. "Just how did you come to be known as night hawk?"

His eyes downcast, this unexpected attention made the kid blush. Until now, his grimy fingers hovered over polished silverware. He watched others without taking a bite of food himself. After a moment he picked up the largest fork, perhaps thinking if he were busy, he would not have to respond to questions.

"I can answer that, Rose," Major Lange said.

She raised her hand to silence him. "No, no. I want this

young man to tell me. My question is simple enough for him to answer without prompting. Speak up, young man."

Everyone stared at the kid while awaiting his answer. He gazed at the fork. Holding the gleaming tines over the pastry shell, he stared down at a brown mass on his plate that looked for all the world like a fresh deposit in a horse pasture.

"Well?" An expression of deep irritation crossed Rose's face with the dawning realization that the kid had no intention of answering her.

Instead, he put the fork down and cast a helpless look at Ty. "I ain't gonna eat this god-damned piece of crap," he said.

A collective gasp from the sisters startled the kid. They glowered at him, their faces tight with anger. Even the host was thunderstruck. Major Lange regarded the kid. The sheriff and his wife averted their eyes, struggling to repress the slightest hint of levity. Smitty looked downward, unmoving.

In a glance Ty could see that the kid knew he had done something wrong, but at once did not know what else he could have done under the circumstances.

"Reckon you'd better leave, son."

The kid pushed his chair back and stood. Half turning, he made his way past the backs of chairs down the length of the dining car. He opened the door and entered the vestibule, turning as he stepped down to ground level. He jogged away, leaving the door standing open.

Smitty took note of this display of bad manners and pushed his chair back. He stood and swiftly followed. Using the occasion to let himself out of the Pullman car, he stepped into the vestibule and closed the door behind him without looking back.

Front Street was illuminated by oil-fueled lamps mounted on posts. By their light Ty caught a glimpse of Smitty through a side window of the dining car. The ranch hand crossed the tracks. He headed for town, Ty figured, to catch up with the kid.

Dinner ended as it had begun—in strained quietude. After devouring the rum-soaked cake, the men filed into Major Lange's domain, a parlor car for his use only. Seated in a cushioned armchair, Ty was reminded of the large vault in the Coalton bank when Lange opened a floor safe to gain access to his humidor.

Ty happened to be seated at an angle that allowed him a glimpse inside this black vault. He saw stacks of cash a moment before Lange closed the heavy door and spun the dial.

In conversation Major Lange asked about crime and bands of outlaws in the region. Rogers answered in detail as Ty looked on. He smoked and relaxed. He figured questions about the Circle L would come tomorrow. After partaking of snifters of brandy and smoking cigars in the parlor car, Ty shook hands with his host. He thanked him for a fine and memorable evening, a half lie repeated by Sheriff Rogers.

Unable to decide if he should offer some excuse for the kid's behavior, Ty elected to invoke a time-honored principle—*The less said, the better.*—and he let it go. Before parting, he agreed to meet Major Lange at Bertha's café in the morning. After breakfast they would go to Jim's livery for the purpose of selling ponies, and then rent a carriage and team for the trip to the ranch.

The sheriff's wife had passed the time in the dining car with her knitting while the servants washed porcelain, cleaned crystal, and polished silver. Excluded from the male custom of a stiff drink and a long smoke after dinner, the sisters retired to their car, leaving Elizabeth to wait alone. She had passed the time knitting a woolen scarf, and hastily put her needles and yarn away when her husband entered from the parlor car. He was accompanied by Ty. The three of them left the car.

With her husband helping her across the tracks outside, she spoke in a bemused tone of voice. "That was quite an exhibition, now, wasn't it?"

"Exhibition?" the sheriff repeated. His tone of voice indicated he had not seen it that way, at all. "You mean that kid mouthing off during dinner?"

"I mean everything about dinner this evening," she said. "I suppose there is something to be said for certainty."

Rogers looked at his wife questioningly. "What?"

She smiled. "I mean that boy certainly knows he will not eat road apples with his dinner."

Ty grinned as she laughed softly. He did not know Elizabeth Rogers well, having met her on only a few occasions in town. She was a tall, rangy woman with dark hair combed smartly upward, pinned in a style that swept under the brim of her hat. Of firm demeanor, she impressed him as one who was not easily rattled—a trait, Ty figured, required for the wife of a lawman.

"When that scrawny kid landed here," Sheriff Rogers went on, "he was two-thirds starved. I found him scrounging out of back alley garbage pails. Didn't I, Ty? You saw him."

The ramrod nodded.

"Now he's a picky eater in a rich man's private dining car," Rogers said. "That's not all."

Ty watched the lawman reach into his coat pocket. He drew out a handbill and thrust it toward him. "I didn't mention it in front of the kid," Rogers said, "but this is what I wanted to talk to you about."

Elizabeth asked: "What is it, Wade?"

"Reward dodger," the lawman replied. "It came in the U.P. mail car a couple weeks ago."

Ty took the handbill from him and stepped closer to the lamplight emanating from a street lamp. He slanted the dodger toward the light as he read it.

WANTED
$1000 Reward
For the capture and arrest of
Jonathan Blake
age 16, brown hair, about 5'6" in stature
Wanted for the murder of Miss Jane Morgan
Death by stabbing in Denver, Colorado
April 17, 1894
Forward all information to Aaron Hayes
United States Marshal, Denver Colorado

Ty looked at Sheriff Rogers. "You figure this is the kid?"

"Could be," Rogers replied. "Sure as hell."

Ty considered that notion, and read the handbill again. Mrs. Rogers leaned closer to him as she read it, too.

"Wade," she said, "this description fits a slew of youngsters."

Her husband jabbed his index finger at the handbill. "Says here the victim was stabbed."

"Most boys carry a knife of some kind or other," she said.

The sheriff countered: "Most boys go by their right names, too."

Ty asked: "What do you aim to do?"

"Question him," Rogers replied. He added pointedly: "If I can find him."

Ty caught the hint. "Smitty took him under his wing. Locate my top hand, and the kid won't be far away, likely."

"Obliged," Rogers said.

Ty added: "The Comet is a good place to start."

"If he's anywhere near Coalton," the lawman said, "I'll get a loop on him."

Mrs. Rogers reached out and grasped her husband's thick arm in both hands. "We've had enough adventure for one night, Wade. It's late. Let's go home. Your night deputy can handle this chore." She cast a parting smile at the ramrod. "Good evening, Ty."

" 'Evening, ma'am."

At sunup Ty met Major Lange in Bertha's café. He introduced him to the proprietress, and learned something new about her. Bertha had shirt-tail relatives in Maryland. After determining none of their relatives had crossed paths in Whitmoor or its luxurious environs, she took meal orders and retreated to her kitchen.

After breakfast Ty and Major Lange crossed the street and followed the plank walk to the livery barn. While Lange looked on, Ty negotiated a price for the mustangs roped and brought in to the Circle L by ranch hands over a period of months. He asked $3.50 for each one, and $8 for a solid color stallion, an American horse never branded.

Ty had included the stallion as a ploy to encourage Jim to bid on the bunch as a means of acquiring one good saddle mount. The wild stallion was worth significantly more than $8, but he figured the ponies were worth less than $3.50 each. After the usual recriminations and howls of pain, he accepted the deal offered by Jim.

Major Lange rented a Rawson & Brothers Overland carriage and a team. With its hickory spokes, heavy axles, and iron rims on the wheels, Jim assured him the stout construction of the vehicle was up to the rigors of a prairie crossing. Seats of tufted leather were mounted on leaf springs, offering cushioned comfort for the ladies.

From there, Ty walked to the bank with Major Lange at his side. He introduced him to Arthur Blaine, and deposited the proceeds of the sale horses in the Circle L account. Ty seized on the occasion to examine the pass book, check stubs, and every computation pertinent to Circle L accounts at the bank.

"Every t is crossed," Major Lange declared as he shook hands with Blaine in parting, "and every i dotted. I would expect no less from Mister Tyler Johnson or his banker. A pleasure to meet you, sir."

"The pleasure is mine," Blaine said. "I assure you."

"Thank you, sir," he said. "Good day."

"And good day to you," the banker said.

On Front Street Major Lange departed and headed for the siding. Ty was joined by Corny when the ranch cook drove the chuck wagon from the mercantile. He hauled back on the lines. Smitty followed on horseback.

"Where's our night hawk?" Ty asked.

Smitty drew rein. Shoving his hat up on his head, he squinted against the glare of the morning sun. "Damned if I know."

Corny adopted an I-told-you-so tone of voice when he announced: "Looks like your night hawk flew the coop, Ty."

Ty turned to Smitty. "He was sticking close to you."

"Until last night, he was," Smitty allowed. "I tried to find him. No sign of him anywhere in this burg. Not last night, not this morning." He added: "No sign of the roan, either."

The longest two days of his life finally ended when Ty topped the grassy rise overlooking the headquarters of the Circle L Ranch. This view in its entirety—stock ponds, garden plots, fenced pastures, haystacks, pole corrals with water troughs, white-washed outbuildings, the towering barn, and the ranch house itself—lent satisfaction in full measure.

With all in order on the home place, his sense of accomplishment never failed to bring a surge of memories. He invariably thought back to his life while working on numerous ranches, starting with his teen years when he had signed on as a wrangler for the Bar 10 in Wyoming. The renowned ranch was a big one, well stocked and well maintained, and proved to be an excellent training ground that guided him later in life.

Ty turned in the saddle. He looked back at the odd little caravan. Driven by Major Lange, the carriage was followed by the chuck wagon, with Corny holding the lines. On horseback, Smitty brought up the rear. He spurred his saddle mount, and, when he caught up with Ty, he drew rein.

At the crest Major Lange hauled back on the lines. He ardently looked past Ty and Smitty, straining for his first glimpse of the ranch headquarters. Having taken on mythical proportions in his imagination, the Circle L was a place that until now had lived in his mind.

Necks craned, Rose and Sharon peered ahead from their seats in the carriage. Wearing long dusters, cuffed gloves, and scarves snugly tied, both ladies lifted a hand to a hat brim in a gesture that might have been a salute of sorts.

The moment passed, and Ty knew from their crestfallen expressions that the gesture was no salute. If they had been promised an estate on the order of a Monticello of the West with tall trees and formal gardens in one of Major Lange's flights of fancy, then they were keenly disappointed.

They *were* keenly disappointed.

"This is your so-called ranch?" Rose demanded of Major Lange.

"It's . . . it's run-down," Sharon said.

"A trash heap," Rose said. "Nothing but a trash heap."

Ty's jaw clenched while Major Lange remained silent. He knew he should have expected nothing less from the sisters. The trip had been a disaster from the start. Rose and Sharon had reacted with outrage when they pried the truth out of Major Lange. The fact that they faced a two-day journey across the prairie, instead of one day, was a deception they took to be a lie and an insult. Neither of the ladies had ever slept under the stars, and, when they discovered that was their fate, Rose demanded to be escorted back to the rail car immediately—even if that meant driving the team all night back to Coalton.

At once they knew that option was impossible. Men and horses were tired and hungry. As a means of venting hot anger, Rose complained bitterly and continuously, her nostrils flaring like a horse under quirt. Sharon blotted tears with her handkerchief. For the first time Ty realized neither woman had brought a change of clothing or any toiletries.

Their conflict reached a boiling point. With any last semblance of Victorian manners cast aside, Rose issued threats to Major Lange. The future of their relationship was as bleak as this prairie, and she did not care who knew it. From an explosion of anger to resolute silence, she glowered at her husband-never-to-be.

90

Instead of fueling their argument, Major Lange cocked his head and directed her attention to the sounds of birds calling. Such calls had distracted her earlier. Now, however, not even the melodious trills of red-winged blackbirds softened her mood. Worse, for Major Lange to suggest she could be so easily influenced only deepened her rage.

The three men fashioned a bed from sougans unrolled from the chuck wagon. They tried to make the ladies comfortable for a night's rest while they themselves slept on the hard ground without cover.

Darkness fell. Even though a campfire blazed, Rose and Sharon were frightened by coyotes, unseen and yipping in the night. Rose demanded one of the men stay awake all night to protect them.

Ty assured her the prairie wolves were harmless. He did not say so aloud, but he was more concerned a snake might slither into a warm shoe or a lizard skitter under a sougan. In the morning while Corny prepared breakfast, Ty shook out the ladies' foot gear and bedding—only to draw an accusation of impropriety.

"You are not to touch my belongings, Mister Johnson," Rose said, snatching a high-button shoe from his grasp. "Not under any circumstances are you to touch any article of my clothing. Do you understand?"

"He meant no harm, Rose," Major Lange said wearily, earning another withering look from eyes that blazed.

Now Ty took the lead and descended the slope to the ranch headquarters. He had taken offense at the behavior of both women, but kept his thoughts to himself as he wondered why Major Lange was betrothed to either sister.

To his eye, the Circle L was not run-down. Far from it. The ranch house was tight. So was the bunkhouse. The outbuildings and the horse barn were in excellent condition, each with a full complement of bull snakes. Stock ponds were full, pastures green.

Approaching the yard on horseback, Ty saw Dean Bowles and George Taylor. They were in the corral with the wild mare and her foal. The ranch hands must have heard vehicles coming, for both men ducked out of the corral, hands on their hips as they waited by the water trough. When Ty reined up, the two men eyed the carriage and passengers coming along behind him.

"Howdy, gents," Ty said. "Looks like you've been working."

Turning to the ramrod, Dean and George greeted him. They informed him of their efforts to tame the mare. She would take a saddle and a bridle now, Dean reported, but shoving a boot in the stirrup to mount was still the beginning of an adventure. The mare no longer tried to kill anyone who got too close to her foal, and that was viewed as a sign of progress in gentling her down.

Ty's eye was caught by a horse in another corral. It was the roan. Moments later a solitary figure emerged from barn shadows. Ty saw the kid step into full daylight.

Chapter Six

At that moment Ty realized he was in possession of information unknown to anyone else on the Circle L. He alone knew Sheriff Rogers suspected the handbill had named the kid as a murderer, a killer sought by federal marshals stationed in Denver.

Ty considered taking the kid aside to find out if he answered to the name of Jonathan Blake. Upon reflection, though, he figured the kid would run if spooked. For that reason he did not mention the name or the sheriff's theory. After all, he was abiding by an unwritten code among ranchers. While criminals were rarely sheltered on a ranch, by custom it was up to lawmen to pursue and apprehend fleeing fugitives. The ramrod and his ranch hands were not expected to capture, subdue, or grill a desperate man. A man's back trail was his business, no one else's.

Ty did not see the boot coming, but knew he should have after Major Lange poked his nose into the ranch house, the barn, the bunkhouse, and even the outbuildings. After consulting Rose and Sharon, Lange promptly announced the two women would take up residence in the ranch house. They would move in as soon as the windows were covered to protect their privacy.

Ty got the boot. He lugged his bedding and war bag to the bunk in the tack room in the barn. In the meantime, Rose demanded "that skunk's den" of a ranch house be swept, mopped, and fumigated, thoroughly cleaned from the ratty bearhide on the floor to countless spider webs lacing the ceiling.

So advised, Ty crossed the verandah and entered the ranch house with broom in hand. He looked around for a moment, confirming his opinion that this place did not look too bad or smell too bad, either. Furnishings were rough-hewn, but to his liking. So was the decor—a pair of Texas longhorns, elk and deer antlers, a weathered buffalo skull, and a rifle—all of them mounted on the walls opposite a potbelly stove. A hurricane lamp hung from a length of wire looped around the ridge pole. Directly under it, an arm-chair on casters had been shoved up against a roll-top desk.

On the desk stood a photographic portrait of a young woman and a baby. With the infant in her arms, a slight smile identified the woman as the mother. Her gaze came out of the past, for the moment holding Ty's attention.

More than an office, more than a bunk behind a blanket suspended from rafters, this was Ty's domain. No women and few men had ever seen it. Circle L cowhands were relegated to their quarters in the bunkhouse or to the ranch house verandah where they smoked, chewed, and spat while cussing and discussing pressing issues.

The desk top and the floor around it were covered with yellowed newspapers and magazines. Added to the heap were brass shell casings, parts for traps, three old guns, pieces of tanned leather, and a Barlow pocket knife with one blade broken—items that "just might come in handy someday."

Ty had no stomach for moving anything or tidying up

the place. He knew where everything was, and he knew why he had kept them. His possessions included pencils and a ledger with a dozen pages torn out. Not litter, but years of collecting had made this place what it was. The more he thought about getting the boot, the more he considered his options. He disliked all of the choices open to him. He was about two inches away from packing his war bag and drawing his time when Major Lange entered the ranch house. Ty listened to his apology.

"I know it comes hard," Lange said, glancing around. "This has been your home for a good long time, and out of the blue you have been displaced by two women mad as hornets." Lange's gaze lingered on the portrait of the mother and child. The edges of the portrait were smudged from fingers holding it over the years. For a moment Lange seemed ready to ask about it. Then he shifted his gaze to Ty.

"Am I correct in my assessment of your state of mind?"

Ty nodded.

"You may be interested to know," Lange went on, "that I have devised a plan. Will you do me the favor of hearing me out?"

"I'll listen."

"As you may have guessed," Lange said, "Rose and Snapdragon are keen to begin their journey back to Coalton. First thing in the morning, they will depart. All I need from you is a driver. Either the cook or that range rider named Smitty . . . both are capable and sober men, I presume." Lange tugged at his beard. "Upon their departure, you and I shall tour Circle L range land and observe my cattle and horse herds. Once that task is completed, I shall return to the Coalton siding. From there, the ladies and I will travel by rail back to Whitmoor, post haste."

Lange paused again. "This plan is agreeable to the

ladies. Does it suit you?"

Ty did not answer immediately.

"You have misgivings?" Lange asked.

"Reckon I do," Ty said.

"Such as?"

"I aimed for Smitty to ride with us," Ty said. "And Corny needs to stay here on the home place."

"Why does Smitty need to go with us?" Lange asked. "You know the boundaries of this ranch property as well as anyone."

"Smitty's the only hand," Ty replied, "who can take us straight to a marsh where Circle L steers are holed up. I figured he'd help us round up those four-legged outlaws. We'll make a drive and bring them in. I've got a cutting horse for you to ride. Western saddle, too."

Major Lange smiled at the prospect of herding steers across the great prairie of the American West. He was at once troubled, though. "What about Cornelius? Surely he can drive the carriage."

Ty shook his head. "Corny has work to do here."

"But who else can possibly undertake this task?" Lange asked, and quickly answered his own question. "Not that ill-tempered youngster, the one you call night hawk?"

"The kid has chores to do hereabouts," Ty replied. "Corny will make sure they get done."

"I see," Major Lange said. "But I dare say the ladies cannot handle a team of horses by themselves."

Ty jerked a thumb toward the bunkhouse. "Two of my ranch hands are still on the place . . . Dean Bowles and George Taylor. After they collect their pay, they'll head back to Coalton. No reason they can't drive that carriage."

"Two range riders," Major Lange said in a measured tone. "No offense intended, Ty, but your riders are a bit rough around the edges."

"The men who work here have to be rough around the edges," Ty said, "to get along with the ramrod."

"I appreciate your humor, Ty," he said. "But I must ask . . . can you vouch for their character as honorable gentlemen?"

"Reckon I can."

Lange pondered this notion. "Your endorsement is good enough for me. I know you don't take this lightly. What the ladies will think of the arrangement, I can only guess. They will complain mightily, I suppose. They have complained about everything else since we crossed the Missouri. We can only hope their eagerness to depart outweighs their misgivings . . . which I expect to be vociferous." He waved a hand around the room. "Finish sweeping and straighten the place up a bit more. As soon as the windows are covered, the king's palace will be ready to receive two princesses."

Ty grinned, relieved to have cleared the air.

"As you may have surmised," Major Lange confided, "marriage to Rose is no longer a certainty in my future. Oh, the ill will is primarily my fault. I know that now. I should never have brought Rose and her sister. I was intent on touring my ranch with them serving as my witnesses. I meant to silence doubters back home once and for all. I could think of nothing else. A foolish plan, wasn't it?" He drew a breath. "I should have told Rose the truth to start with. I would have, but I knew she would never consent to a two-day crossing of the wild prairie. I thought I could get her out of that Pullman car and coax her along, one pretty prairie flower or one melodious bird call at a time. The notion was born of a lie."

Major Lange paused in thought. "Perhaps that is destined to be the greatest lesson of this journey for me."

Ty straightened the desk, picked up papers, and shook out

the bear rug. He raised clouds of dust and rolled out dead flies and the carcasses of miller moths when he swept the plank floor to the open doorway. After sweeping the verandah, he tacked burlap sacks over the window frames to cover the panes. Why anyone would cut off a view of the home ranch and a fine expanse of prairie was beyond his understanding.

While working at these onerous tasks, he picked up the portrait from the desk. Holding it before him, he gazed at the image of a young woman holding her baby. He heard footfalls on the verandah, and turned. The kid moved into the doorway.

"Howdy," Ty said.

Hat in hand, the kid peered into the main room of the ranch house. It was dimly lit. He had never ventured in, and he did not cross the threshold now, either.

"I aim to ride with you."

"Ride where?" Ty asked.

"You know where," the kid said.

"Reckon you'll have to tell me, son," Ty said.

"Circle L range," he said. "Top to bottom. I aim to ride with you and that dude, Lange."

Ty shook his head. "I'm taking Smitty. I want you to stay here and get after your chores." He added: "Do what Corny tells you."

Lips pursed, the kid said: "Hell, I might as well quit you. I ain't doing no good here."

"Your time will come," Ty said.

"When?"

"When I tell you."

"Like I said, I might as well quit you."

Ty set the straw broom aside and moved into the doorway. Looking past the kid, he pointed across the yard to the mare confined in the pole corral.

"All right. Mount up."

Surprised, the kid said: "Huh?"

"I told you that mare is yours if you can ride her," Ty said. "Stay aboard long enough to work out the kinks, and you can ride with us on your horse."

The kid's gaze swung to the corral adjoining the barn, and back to Ty again. "Trying to get me killed?"

"I'd say you have the advantage."

"How do you figure that?"

"Dean and George worked with that mare while we were gone," Ty replied. "Far as I know, she's ready for the saddle. My offer stands. Take it or leave it."

Backed into a corner of his own making, the kid nodded curtly. Without a word, he wheeled and set out for the corral.

The ruckus drew a crowd that included Rose and Sharon. The ladies scowled as they waved away clouds of dust and a haze of dried manure dust kicked up by the mare. When Major Lange joined them, the three ranch hands—Dean, George, and Smitty—leaned against the top rail, looking on.

Rope in hand, the kid pursued the mare, first at a wary walk, then on the run. The kid was clumsy. He was led on a merry chase, a comical contest that the mare could have played all day. Hearing the laughter of onlookers and seeing the hopelessness of his pursuit, the kid halted. He threw the rope down, and spun around to face Ty.

"Hell, this ain't fair," the kid said. "Not by a long shot."

"How's that?" Ty asked.

"You said it," the kid said. "Two men saddled this wild horse. It can't be done by me alone. You knew that all along, didn't you?"

Ty replied evenly: "I know what any wrangler and night hawk should know."

"Huh?" the kid asked.

"A horse can out-dodge a man," Ty said.

The kid swore, raising more dust when he kicked at the rope.

Ty lifted a hand and caught the attention of Dean and George. "Catch her, boys. Catch her, and snub her down for the night hawk."

The two ranch hands ducked under a rail and stepped into the corral. Dean bent down and picked up the rope. He coiled it while George held his hat aloft and gradually hazed the mare to the far side of the corral. The moment came when she felt trapped and broke for the other side, foal close behind. The mare ran straight into a loop gently tossed by Dean. He hauled back on the rope, spun it around the post, and in a matter of seconds the horse was snubbed in the middle of the pole corral.

Squealing and kicking, she finally gave up the fight. With her chest heaving and head hanging, the mare took the bridle. After a few perfunctory kicks, she accepted the blanket and the saddle. George cinched it and stepped back.

Ty nodded. "She's all yours, night hawk."

The kid made his way into the corral and stepped to the left side of the mare. He hopped and climbed aboard, only to be pitched the moment the cowhands loosened the rope and let go. Landing hard on his buttocks, the kid grimaced as he fought tears.

Ty nodded at the ranch hands. They helped the kid mount, and stood back to watch. Seeing him thrown again, the ladies giggled as though observing a circus act. A third attempt ended with the same result. Amid peals of laughter the kid limped away. He approached Ty standing outside the corral.

"You son-of-a-bitch."

Rose and Sharon gasped. With a horrified glance at one another, the women stepped back, turned, and fled like a pair of flushed doves. They did not take flight, but the ladies held their skirts out of the dirt as they hurried along, arms bent at the elbows, wing-like. Mounting four stairs, they crossed the verandah and rushed into the ranch house.

Ty saw the door close. He glanced at Smitty and jabbed his thumb toward the kid. "I'm getting a fair idea of why you lit into him, bare-fisted, like you did."

Smitty answered with a grin.

The kid ducked through the corral rails. He straightened and glowered at Ty, tears streaming from his eyes now.

"I swore at you, Mister Ramrod. I cussed you proper. You gonna whup me? You gonna cut me loose? What's it gonna be?"

When Ty did not answer, the kid pressed him. "Whatcha gonna do, Mister Ramrod?"

Ty said: "Give you a choice."

"Choice," the kid repeated. "What the hell do you mean by that? What kinda choice?"

"You can walk from here to Coalton blubbering like a baby," Ty said, "or you can stay on the Circle L and learn what it takes to be a man."

"What the hell are you jawing about?"

"Think about it, son," Ty said. "You're plumb afoot. The only way you'll earn a horse and saddle to call your own is to stick." He added: "Smitty already told you that, didn't he? Listen to him."

The kid muttered another string of curses.

"Keep that up," Ty said, "and I'll take you behind the woodshed myself. If you think Smitty took you down a notch, wait till I get done with you. You'll feel like a plow horse walked on you . . . and backed up for a second go-round."

Hastily wiping his eyes, the kid glowered in his anger and frustration. But he did not curse.

The high ridge known among Circle L ranch hands as Ty's Bluff loomed in a starlit sky. At the base of the promontory a campfire blazed.

Ty and Smitty sat cross-legged. Major Lange reclined on an elbow. They smoked Lange's cigars while the horses stood nearby, hobbled. Teamsters favored cigars, Lange informed these cattlemen, and the term stogie was derived from Conestoga, the big freight outfits that supplied settlers in the West before steel.

While the men smoked, Ty recounted the circumstances of the death of Bill Connors, confirming details from Smitty. As it turned out, a cousin of Major Lange's had suffered a similar fate half a dozen years ago—thrown from a jumping horse, the man's neck was broken when he landed on the turf. Through all of these years since that accident, Lange had blamed the lightweight English saddle favored by his cousin in jumping competitions. He was surprised to learn Bill Connors was mounted on a Western saddle. With its bigger horn and more leather to grasp than the English counterpart, still he had been pitched.

It had happened fast, Smitty reported. The speed of the charging steer left no time for Bill to grab the horn or anything else to hang on to for dear life. As he vividly recalled, his partner had been propelled out of the saddle, thrown with little or no warning.

"Sometimes a man just don't stand a chance," Smitty said. "No chance a-tall."

They smoked and talked late into the night. Major

Lange looked skyward and demonstrated a seaman's knowledge of the constellations. He described a solitary childhood of gazing into the heavens after daylight hours of tutoring by demanding teachers. Force-fed names, dates, and places, he studied the subjects of Greek literature, Latin, and the long and murderous history of Europe from Huns and Goths to the era of warring Germanic city-states.

Major Lange's upbringing in Whitmoor and his classical education was just about as foreign to Ty and Smitty as it could possibly be, but the stars were the same here as the pinpoints of celestial lights reflected on the waters of Chesapeake Bay. As owls hooted, the ramrod listened to Lange while he thought about that. Presently a coyote yipped, echoed by another. Bats darted through the sky like night shadows. Unseen by men, the calls of nocturnal predators were answered by members of their species. Survival guided them all, Ty thought, and some would not live through the night.

By the time they rolled out sougans and positioned saddles on the ground for headrests, Ty felt a stronger connection to Major Lange. In his eyes, the gent was no longer an effete dude washed up from the Maryland shore to the Colorado prairie, no longer an insane man who stood before him in the Coalton House proclaiming the death of his mother.

They broke camp at dawn. Smitty led the way northward. The ride was a long one. After numerous stops to rest and water the horses, the sun was low in the western sky when Smitty drew rein. He raised his hand as Ty and Major Lange halted beside him.

Smitty pointed to a bald rise in the prairie. Small birds filled the sky overhead. So did clouds of insects. A scent of water filled the air. Turning in the saddle, Smitty spoke in a low tone.

"Me and Bill, we found the marsh on the other side of this hill . . . standing water and plenty of grass. Surprised the hell out of us. When Bill spied all that grass, he claimed the whole spread for himself."

Alarmed, Major Lange turned to Ty. "This is Circle L range, isn't it?"

"From here to the Wyoming line," Ty assured him.

"A cowhand's gotta dream of something besides women, don't he?" Smitty asked.

Leaving their mounts hobbled in a patch of grass, they walked upslope toward the crest. When they drew near, they dropped to their knees and inched closer. Ty crawled with them and lay prone on sun-warmed soil. Just as Smitty had described it, this low hill overlooked a natural wetland. It was choked with brush and fringed by grass. The sheen of water down there was an unexpected sight on the dry prairie.

Beyond the marshland Ty saw the remains of a homesteader's cabin. Long abandoned and nearly taken over by this expanse of low vegetation, weathered boards had warped and split, the dirt roof caved in. A plank door dangled from leather straps that had once served as hinges.

Ty glimpsed movement. He turned and saw pronghorn, twenty or more, turn tail and bound away. He looked around. No sign of cattle from this vantage point. In reply to his whispered question, Smitty pointed to a stand of brush beyond the marsh.

"The steers favor cool shade over yonder."

He had no sooner spoken than branches moved, swaying back and forth. Like a beast suddenly come to life, one brawny steer emerged from the thicket. He was followed by others. The leader lumbered to shallow water, lowered his head, and drank.

Ty counted fourteen beeves. As far as he could determine, all of them bore the Circle L brand. One must have caught a foreign scent or was spooked by a strange sight. Raising his head, water ran from his jowls as he looked directly at the crest of the hill where three men lay on their bellies, watching. The steer turned and beat a swift retreat. Followed by the other outlaws, he disappeared in the thicket.

"Wild as deer," Ty observed.

Smitty nodded. "And twice as jumpy. Me and Bill, we just about busted two good horses heading up them miserable go-backers."

"Looks like we've got our work cut out for us, gents," Ty said. He gestured toward the cabin. "We'll see about bunching them in the morning. For now we'll make camp by that shipwreck over there."

Major Lange smiled as he gazed at the weathered remains of the cabin. "Resembles a beached boat, doesn't it? I suppose the poet would compare this prairie to a vast sea with waves forever standing in place." He added: "A traveler's delight, a sailor's nightmare."

A short distance away, Ty discovered imprints in the soft soil. He knelt, his fingertips touching shallow depressions.

"What is it, Ty?" Major Lange asked.

"Two sets of hoofs," he replied. "Large and small."

"Me and Bill," Smitty said, "we never came this way."

"A saddle horse and pack animal left these tracks," Ty said.

"Fresh?" Smitty asked.

He looked up at him and shook his head. "Trail's cold."

Smitty grinned. "Cold as yesterday's pancakes, as Corny says."

Lange smiled upon hearing a colorful expression new to him.

Head bowed, Ty followed the tracks. The dim trail took him past the ruined cabin to a fire ring and the dark ashes of a campfire. Bottles and empty tins were scattered about the site.

Ty turned to Smitty. "I'm just thinking."

"Thinking what?" he asked.

"Bill was spooked by a lone rider on the home place a while back," Ty said.

Smitty nodded. "A stranger leading a pack mule. The gent didn't tarry. He took supper dished up by Corny, grained his animals, and moved on without saying more than three words. Bill hid in the barn the whole time."

Major Lange asked: "Was your rider fleeing the law?"

Smitty shrugged. "Me and Bill, we rode side-by-side, but he never mentioned nothing about his back trail. Nary a word."

"Tight-lipped, was he?" Lange asked.

Smitty nodded once. "You could say that."

"Seems to me," Lange observed, "I could say that about most of you Westerners."

Morning dawned with a frosty chill in the air. Ty made a discovery when Smitty stepped away from camp to relieve himself. He heard Smitty call out. With Major Lange following, he found the ranch hand standing over a coal seam.

Ty looked around. The earth had been disturbed.

It was apparent that a pick and shovel had been used to excavate a series of shallow trenches. The trenches radiated out from a black seam some 200 feet wide. One probe was a deep hole in the ground that had exposed more coal. Other excavations were marked by wooden stakes. The digger was clearly exploring an anthracite deposit, and he had endeavored to estimate the length, breadth, and depth of it.

"Coal prospector," Ty said, shaking his head as he examined boot prints in dry soil.

"That stranger who came through the home ranch wasn't a lawman or bounty hunter," Smitty said. "He was a prospector. Bill didn't have nothing to worry over, did he? Nothing a-tall."

Ty nodded in mute agreement, but he was thinking about something else. "I recollect seeing a canvas cover lashed to the stranger's pack saddle."

"Yeah, I saw it, too," Smitty said.

"I figured it was a case for a hunting rifle," Ty went on. "More likely, it covered the legs of a tripod."

"Tripod?" Lange repeated.

"For a surveyor's transit," Ty replied.

Smitty added: "He could have been hiding a pick and shovel in there, too."

Major Lange gazed at the coal deposit exposed by spaded prairie soil. "Pardon my ignorance, gentlemen, but what does this have to do with a cattle ranch?"

"It means a prospector was trespassing on your land," Ty said. "You own all rights, mineral and water, above or below ground to this ranch. Some gent came here to take measurements."

"For what reason?" Lange asked.

"Since he didn't ask permission to dig when he had the chance," Ty answered, "I'd say he aimed to find out if enough coal is here to make it worthwhile to sink a shaft."

"You mean to mine coal?" Lange asked. "Without permission?"

Ty nodded. He turned and gazed toward the horizon. "A man could run wagons from here to Laramie and sell coal to the U.P. in Wyoming . . . without ever tipping you off or anyone else."

Lange turned his attention to Ty. "This is a big ranch. How can we stop thievery of this kind?"

"Circle L riders keep an eye peeled for sign," Ty replied. "Fact is most strangers are passing through on their way to Wyoming, honest men hunting deer or elk. If a gent gets contrary on us, my riders have permission to persuade him to change his ways."

"Persuade," Lange repeated, eyebrows arched. "You mean, lynch him."

Ty and Smitty exchanged a glance.

"The West isn't quite that wild these days," Ty said. "But we just might show a rope to get a man's attention before sending him on his way to the nearest property line."

Major Lange looked around. "I am wondering about that, too."

"Wondering about what?" Ty asked.

"You were talking about the state line dividing Colorado and Wyoming," he said. "Where is it?"

Ty waved a hand northward. "Over yonder."

"But where . . . precisely?"

"Reckon I don't know that," Ty said. "We'd have to roll out maps in the land office in Coalton to find out."

"Then that is what we shall do," Lange said.

Three strong, highly trained horses were needed to herd fourteen outlaw steers to pasture. A fight all the way, every day, the riders were not so much herding domestic animals as they were chasing wild beasts. Hills were dotted with obstacles in the form of prairie dog dens, clumps of pear cactus, sage, and ravines choked with brush.

Ty noted Major Lange was an experienced horseman who was smart enough to let the horse work. Having never ridden a cutting horse before, Lange grabbed the saddle horn and held on, pulling hard enough to yank it out by the roots, as cowhands described a greenhorn sticking on an agile horse. Lange stayed in the saddle while his mount dived left or dodged right to head off bunch quitters.

Tired and caked with trail dust by the time they reached their destination, the three men craved baths, chow, and a warm night's sleep. Time pauses for no man, Ty knew, and he felt his age when one sougan did not provide enough insulation against the chill of autumn nights in the great outdoors, not the way a blanket once did when he was riding the range.

On the home place they turned their saddle horses into the corral. With no sign of the kid, Smitty tended the horses while Ty and Major Lange checked the ranch house. Finding it empty and all too clean and orderly, they mounted a brief search for the kid. He was not in the horse barn, bunkhouse, or outbuildings.

Ty's shouts were answered by Corny. The ranch cook stepped out of his shack abutting the far end of the mess hall. Wiping his hands on a towel fashioned from cotton flour sacks, Corny assured Major Lange the ladies had departed for Coalton with Dean and George driving the carriage, as planned.

"Where's the night hawk?" Ty demanded.

"Sheriff Rogers came and took him," Corny answered.

Ty stared at him in amazement. "Took him?"

Corny nodded. "Rogers showed up here a couple days ago. He put your night hawk in irons and took him to Coalton on that sway-backed roan."

Chapter Seven

"One of these damned days I'm gonna kill me a man! God-damned if I ain't! Might as well kill me a man, the way I'm treated in these parts! Leastways I'll get hanged for a reason!"

The kid's hair was tousled, his pimpled face flushed and shining with sweat. Ty watched him grab the iron bars, knuckles turning white as though he intended to yank them out with his bare hands. Ty did not tell him, but bigger, stronger men had tried.

Amid stale odors of urine and chaw, the ramrod looked on impassively outside the cell door. He had seen and smelled the interior of this cell-block many times over the years when he had paid fines to bail out Circle L ranch hands. He freed men who had cut the wolf loose in one saloon after another. Rousted the morning after the night before, most of them whimpered like pups as they begged Ty to spring them and let them ride back to the home ranch, *pronto.*

The kid was neither drunk nor hung over. He was enraged—by his own testimony not mad as hell, but madder than hell. He had royally cursed Sheriff Rogers all the way from the Circle L. Now he aimed his invective at Ty.

The ramrod let him rant. With no other prisoners on this day, they were alone in the jailhouse. Ty figured the kid's murderous curses drifted into the cosmos without effect.

Smitty had been turned away in the sheriff's office. One visitor at a time in the cell-block was the policy here, no exceptions. The last Ty saw, the ranch hand was headed for the Comet.

Ty learned from Sheriff Rogers that the U.P. westbound was bringing a United States Marshal. The marshal accompanied a witness from Denver. The witness had seen a young man commit murder.

"Let me know," Ty said to the kid now, "when you're ready to talk sense."

"Sense! Hell, I'm the only one around here who makes any sense! You don't even know that much, do you, Mister Ramrod?"

Ty backed away. "If that's the way you want it. . . ."

The kid shut his trap and lifted his hands in a gesture of grudging surrender. "What do you want?"

Ty halted. "Answers to some questions."

"What questions?"

"For starters . . . do you go by Jonathan Blake?"

"Hell, no. I told the sheriff."

"What name did your ma give you, then?"

"None of your damned business. Told the sheriff that, too."

Ty studied him. "Did you do it?"

"Do what?" he demanded. "Kill some girl?"

Ty nodded.

"Hell, no!" he said. "I never killed no girl, stabbed or otherwise. I never killed nobody. Never even set foot in Denver."

"Then you don't have anything to worry about," Ty said.

"What do you mean?"

"The witness can't identify you if you've never been to Denver," Ty replied. "Rogers will have to cut you loose."

"What if the witness is wrong?" the kid asked.

Ty thought about that. "Why would he be?"

"A witness can be dead wrong," the kid said. "Or paid off."

"Paid off?"

"It's happened," he insisted.

"How do you know?"

"I read about it in the *Police Gazette*."

Ty shook his head. "Half of those tales are made up."

"What about the other half?" the kid countered. He drew a breath. "A man in Missouri got hanged, lynched for some killing he never done. Nobody found out a witness had been paid off until it was too late. Neck busted from a gallows hanging rope, an innocent man was dead and buried. The liar disappeared, never seen again. I read about it."

Hinges squealed when the cell-block door opened. Ty saw Sheriff Rogers enter. The lawman sported a black, vested suit with a nickel-plated badge pinned to the lapel, his Peacemaker holstered. A big man and full-bearded, the outfit gave him the formidable presence of an officer of the law.

"If you're finished cussing out the ramrod of the Circle L Ranch," Rogers said to the kid, "you can start on me again. I'm rested up, ready for anything you can deal out."

The kid glowered at the sarcasm. "When's that damned train getting in?"

"About three hours," Rogers said. "You might as well spend the time jawing."

"Jawing? Who with? You sure as hell ain't got nothing to say. Neither one of you. All you want is my confession so you can get on with a hanging. Ain't that right, lawman?"

"The gentleman from Maryland," Rogers said.

"Huh?" the kid asked.

Rogers went on: "He wants to talk to you."

The kid's brow arched. "You mean, that dude . . . Major Lange? Why the hell would I give him the time of day?"

"He owns the spread where you draw your pay," Rogers replied with exaggerated patience. "Seems to me, if you are innocent as you claim, then you'd want to tell him you've been falsely accused in this matter."

"I don't have to tell that dude nothing," the kid said dully.

"Not unless you aimed to be courteous," Rogers said, "and show a little respect while you're at it."

"What are you driving at, Mister Lawman?"

"For one thing," Rogers said, "maybe he can help you."

"How?" the kid demanded.

"You'll never know if you don't hear what he has to say."

The kid swore again.

"For another thing," Rogers went on, "you're the reason Major Lange is still in Coalton."

"Me?" the kid said. "How do you figure that?"

"The westbound train carrying a U.S. marshal and a witness has priority," Rogers said. "Lange's Pullman coaches have to stay on the siding, stuck in Stink Water Junction on account of you."

The remark stymied the kid for a long moment. "What the hell. I don't give a damn. Send in the dude."

Ty found Smitty at the bar in the Comet. Over a beer he

recounted the kid's state of mind. He mentioned the hand-bill and cited the sheriff's suspicion regarding the kid's identity.

Ty was aware of Smitty's protracted silence as Ray, the barkeep, wiped the bar down. When Ray moved away in response to a patron's call for alcohol, Ty posed a question to his top hand.

"How do you see this thing, Smitty?"

The ranch hand looked at the mirror where long-necked liquor bottles were lined up shoulder to shoulder like corked soldiers. He turned to him. "I've rode alongside some tough customers over the years, and I keep thinking. . . ."

"Thinking what?"

"I keep thinking the kid ain't the killing kind," Smitty replied. "But I've got a dark feeling he's gonna swing. Can't get it out of my head . . . that kid climbing the steps of a gallows . . . the hangman with a noose waiting for him."

Ty studied him.

Smitty went on: "The kid's a foul-mouthed know-it-all, and he lets fly with threats. But I've never seen him make good on any of them. I ain't proud of what I done to him outside the bunkhouse the day we buried Bill, but the kid never once threatened me or tried to get back at me. Fact is he listened close when I taught him a thing or two about horses. He wanted to learn, and he did learn a few things."

Ty gave these comments some thought. He recalled Sheriff Rogers's earlier characterization. He had said the kid was alone, hungry, and scared. Not mean, the lawman claimed, but scared. Rogers had apparently changed his mind about that. Ty figured it was the handbill that con-

114

vinced him the kid should be arrested, convinced him to make the long ride to the Circle L Ranch and bring his prisoner back in irons.

Ty respected Smitty's views, having heard him hold forth in bunkhouse debates. Now he watched him lift the mug and tip his head back. Draining it, Smitty put the mug down and wiped the back of his hand across his mouth. The sound of batwing doors swinging open drew their attention to the saloon entrance.

Major Lange stepped into the Comet. Crossing the sawdust-covered floor, he made a beeline for Ty and Smitty at the bar.

"Gentlemen," he greeted them, and signaled Ray to set up a round.

Ty leaned on his elbows. Flanked by Smitty and Major Lange, he felt comfortable in their company. Having ridden together and having completed a cattle drive without loss of man or beast lent a sense of trust between them, a mutual respect forged among men. Mettle had been tested, and none had been found wanting.

"You and the kid have yourselves a powwow?" Ty asked now.

"We spoke for a while," Lange answered. A gnome-like smile crossed his face. "Perhaps I should say 'we jawed for a good long spell,' as you Westerners would phrase it."

Ty asked: "What's the verdict?"

"Your chore boy claims innocence," Lange said, and added: "Vehemently."

"You believe him?" Ty asked.

Major Lange replied: "I should think you are better qualified than I to answer that question."

Ty shrugged. "There's an old saying about a gent who can't see the forest for the trees, isn't there?"

"Bring a sharp axe to the task," Major Lange advised him.

Ray brought three beers. He set them before the men and turned away, leaving them to continue their discussion.

"Here's to trail dust, gents," Smitty said, raising a beer mug topped with foam. "Wash it down and keep it down until it turns to mud."

Baffled by another colorful expression new to him, Major Lange echoed the toast without an inkling of knowing what it meant.

Ty turned to him. "What's your guess?"

"About your chore boy's innocence or guilt?"

Ty nodded.

Major Lange addressed the subject after a full measure of deliberation. "His fate hangs in the balance, I should say."

Ty nodded agreement.

"The youngster will live or die," Lange stated, "by the verdict borne on a cloud of coal smoke billowing from the next locomotive, Coalton bound. I should think anyone facing the likelihood of a noose fitted snugly around one's neck would vigorously lay claim to innocence, would he not?"

Ty nodded again, slowly, as he sorted out meaning in the verbiage.

"Oh, he's young and brash as most boys are," Major Lange went on, warming to his subject. "Despite his impudence and numerous shortcomings, the prospect of hanging a youthful criminal is a grim business. Grim, indeed. One would like to believe an errant youngster will find the right path later in life, but at once our demands for justice often outweigh compassion for anyone who has taken a life, particularly in an act of murderous violence. Wouldn't you say?"

Ty replied: "Reckon so."

After another swallow of beer, Lange set the mug down. "You may be interested to know, Ty, that I visited the local Land Office. I gained some valuable information when the agent rolled out his maps."

"What kind of information?" Ty asked.

"For one, that marsh Smitty led us to is on the map," Major Lange said. "So is an old homesteader's claim. Four sections reverted to the state of Colorado twenty-odd years ago." Lange paused. "That coal seam we found is not shown on any map of the region."

Ty eyed him. "You aim to buy it?"

Lange nodded. "I went straight from the Land Office to the telegrapher and notified my bank to transfer funds for the purchase of land, water, and mineral rights of all four sections. Consider the matter settled. The ranch is complete now, complete all the way to the northern boundary where Colorado borders Wyoming." Lange slapped his hands together. "Enough business, gentlemen. Let's have a match, shall we?"

"A match," Smitty said.

Ty was still thinking about that homesteader's claim. It was a fine piece of range land, as Bill Connors had pointed out.

"Match?" Smitty asked Lange. "What kind of match?"

"Croquet," Lange replied.

"Huh?" Smitty said.

"We shall take up mallets," Lange replied, "and whack a ball around while we await the arrival of the west-bound."

"Whackaballaround," Smitty said, running the words together. He cast a questioning look at the ramrod.

Ty answered his unspoken question with a shrug.

Smitty asked Lange: "Just what is this here whack-aballaround?"

"A contest," Major Lange answered. "It is played with mallets and balls. I assure you, there is no better way to pass idle time. The hours fly by as one becomes immersed in the intricacies of the match."

Wary of the unknown, the ramrod and his top hand were hesitant to acquiesce or even to hint at ignorance. From childhood chores to the work of men, they had labored from dawn to dark most of their lives. Livestock did not honor the Sabbath or take a holiday, permitting only rare occasions for men to indulge in frivolous games. The notion of passing time idly was not only foreign to them, but raised suspicions of "idle hands in the workshop of the devil."

"This game," Ty said, speaking with deliberation as he framed his question, "is it anything like checkers?"

Major Lange replied: "No, it's nothing like a board game."

"Horseshoes?" Smitty suggested.

Major Lange shook his head. "Allow me to explain. In the game of croquet each player takes up a mallet. Each player strikes a ball to propel it through a series of wire arches. The arches are called wickets.

"Wicked?" Smitty said.

"No, wick*et*," Lange corrected him. "The player who whacks his ball through all of the wickets and completes the course first wins. Simple as that."

Ty was opposed to gambling. "Wins what?"

"Why, every last morsel of glory from a hard-fought victory," Major Lange said, flashing his gnome-like smile again. "What more could any mortal desire?"

The humor of his remark escaped both the ramrod and the ranch hand. They stared into space, each one trying to conjure up images of the gol'-danged match this Easterner was carrying on about.

Whackaballaround? What the hell kind of loco name is that? Ty wondered.

Lange tugged at his beard. "Rather than depend on me for a description of a game you gentlemen have never seen or played, I propose you accompany me to the vacant lot beside the depot. Edgar will bring all the necessary equipment, and I shall lay out the course while you practice with a mallet and ball. Don't fret, gentlemen. You will learn the game quickly." He added: "After we round everyone up, we shall have ourselves a match."

Ty and Smitty exchanged another glance. *Whackaballaround?*

With sweat-rimmed hats pushed back on their heads, Ty and Smitty watched in silence as the croquet course was laid out in the vacant lot beside the depot. It was defined by wire wickets and pegs pounded into dry prairie soil. Townsfolk had gathered, a few at first. More came as word spread, Elizabeth Rogers among them. Three or four dozen onlookers stood a safe distance away, as though expecting to be beaned by an errant ball.

Major Lange had been right. The game was simple, rules readily learned. Striking a colored ball—red, yellow, orange, brown, blue, or green—with a long-handled mallet bearing a matching color was not difficult. Hitting the ball hard enough to drive it over bumpy ground and through clumps of weeds to a desired spot was.

Ty had not fully understood Major Lange's intent when he declared his "roundup" until Rose and Sharon joined them. Expecting a crowd, the ladies came to play. Even though the autumn day was cool under high, thin clouds, they wore summer whites—long dresses puffed at the sleeves and shaded by beribboned parasols. They were soon joined by the two ranch hands, Dean Bowles and George Taylor.

When Lange had inquired, Ty knew where to find Dean and George. They had been paid the final month's wages with a bonus, and for the moment they were men of means. Last year's lesson was not forgotten. The pair ranged from Bertha's café to the Comet, avoiding gambling dens, deadfalls, and dance halls.

Now Ty heard the ladies greet Dean and George with high-pitched enthusiasm. He noted the ladies no longer looked down their powdered noses while in the presence of bumpkins. The sisters and the two cowhands exhibited a relaxed regard for one another.

Ty figured their changed outlook was the result of two days together at close quarters on their return trip from the Circle L. Toughened up a bit and accustomed to the capricious courses of prairie dust devils, they no longer complained of choking dust or railed against rotten-egg odors emanating from the thermal springs.

In a passing moment Ty saw Rose gaze longingly at Major Lange. Was he jealous? Instead of meeting her gaze, he turned away and knelt to push the last of the croquet wickets into the prairie soil. If she craved his full attention, she received the bare minimum. When balls and mallets were handed out, Lange offered an indifferent gesture to Rose.

"Ladies first," he said curtly.

Elizabeth Rogers stood aside, content to take a place with onlookers rather than play herself. In a manner that was hardly genteel, Rose and Sharon quickly demonstrated their expertise with loud *cracks* of mallets striking balls.

The ranch hands stood back like steers staring at a new gate while the women in white drove their balls away from the first peg through both wickets, earning two more turns. Rose's ball rolled close to the next wicket after firm strikes. Rough as the course was, Sharon followed in fine form.

Ty closely observed the techniques of those who had mastered the game. When his turn came, he struck his blue ball. Clearing the first two wickets, then, after his next shot, his ball came to rest by the green ball struck by Rose. Ty stepped back. He figured the position was a good one. It seemed so until Rose executed a "send".

Ty watched with mounting annoyance. In a sidelong glance he saw a tight-lipped Smitty observe the strategy, too. Instead of hitting her ball to advance to the next wicket, Rose turned. She drew back her mallet, paused, and swung. Her ball rolled up against Ty's. Placing her foot on her ball to hold it firmly, she took a swing. The mallet head struck her ball, hard. The impact sent Ty's ball rolling toward the far end of the course. Observing the success of that maneuver, she laughed in delight.

Ty stared, dumbfounded, while the other players took their turns. In truth, he did not give a hang who won this game. Still, he felt a surge of anger. After her send, he would have to work his way back.

He was not alone for long. As the match progressed, Dean and George fell victim to aggressive play by the sisters. So did Smitty. Even Major Lange was left behind.

Jaw clenched, Ty felt exasperated. He was aware Elizabeth watched him. Polite or not, he tried to exact revenge by striking Rose's ball with his ball. While he could not win, he was eager to make contact and return the favor by driving her ball into the next county. He struck his ball too hard, though, and watched helplessly as it rolled past hers into a tangle of weeds.

Rose and Sharon derided his miscue, their applause muffled by gloved hands. When their turn came, the ladies closed in for the kill on the second half of the course.

Ty worked his way out of the weeds in successive turns, but was never able to close the distance. The ranch hands fared no better, each one easily outdistanced and out-played by the experienced players.

Ty was awaiting his turn when he saw Sheriff Rogers step out of the Union Pacific depot. The lawman clutched a sheet of paper. He waved it over his head when he spotted Ty.

"Westbound's coming," Rogers announced as he closed the distance. Elizabeth left the onlookers and strode to meet her husband.

"Early, isn't it?" she said.

"By two hours," Rogers said. He turned to Ty. "Federal marshal's on board. He's bringing the witness in a private car. I could use a hand, Ty. My night deputies are off duty. They need their sleep."

"Just tell me what to do," Ty said.

Elizabeth listened while her husband held out the paper and explained the contents of the penciled message tele-graphed from the United States Marshal's Office in Denver.

"Says here the witness is a girl of fifteen," he said. "She saw her friend stabbed to death by a footloose kid in Denver. She's still terrified to tears over it. She was too scared to come forward. The marshal talked her into testi-fying by promising to conceal her in a separate car with her mother, windows covered. She can peek out, but no one can see in."

"What do you want me to do?" Ty asked.

"Stand on the platform," he replied, "and help me

122

handle folks, in case a crowd gathers. The marshal wants me to escort the kid onto the platform close to the train car. He figures the witness can get a good look at him without feeling threatened herself."

"Sheriff."

Rogers turned to face Major Lange. "Good day, Mister Lange."

"Good day to you, sir."

"If you will stand back . . . ," Rogers began.

"I couldn't help but overhear," Lange broke in. "May I offer an opinion?"

"Sir, can't you see I'm busy right now . . . ?"

Lange interrupted him. "I do not know if the Circle L night hawk is innocent or guilty of the crime. When I spoke to him in your jailhouse earlier today, he stated his belief that the deck is stacked against him. Having heard what was just said here, I must admit I am inclined to agree with his assessment."

"Mister Lange, I'll thank you to mind your own affairs," Rogers said. "Now, step back, please."

"But, Sheriff. . . ."

This time Rogers interrupted him. "This is a legal matter. It is authorized by order of a United States Marshal. Either the witness recognizes the boy, or she doesn't. It's fair and square."

"Perhaps not."

"What do you mean?"

"If the girl is half as frightened as you indicated," Major Lange said, "consider the scene before her when she arrives."

"Scene? What scene?"

"Put yourself in her place," Lange continued. "Think about what she will see from that train car window."

Rogers paused. "Maybe you ought to tell me."

"She will see a young man bound in irons," Lange explained. "He will be in the custody of a lawman. With that scene before her, she may very well point out the youngster in response to her expectations rather than actually recognizing the murderer."

"We'll have to run that risk," Rogers said.

Lange eyed him. "A young man's life is at stake."

"I am well aware of that fact," Rogers said. "I do not take this lightly."

"I know you don't," Lange said. "I have been here long enough to know you are a fine, upstanding officer of the law. That is why I have a proposal to make, a proposal for justice. Fair and square, as you say. Will you hear me out?"

Rogers cast a doubtful look at him.

"First, take off your badge," Lange said.

"What?" Rogers asked, incredulous.

"And before the train arrives," Lange went on, "release the youngster from irons. Take the restraints away and conceal them."

Rogers stared as though doubting his sanity.

Major Lange gestured toward the three ranch hands standing in the vacant lot with their croquet mallets. "Have those men stand with the night hawk on the platform when the train rolls in. Hats on or off, the witness will have an unbiased opportunity and plenty of time to pick out the guilty man. If she singles out anyone but the night hawk from the Circle L, you'll know she's mistaken. The other men were riding range lands last spring, nowhere near Denver."

Rogers fell silent. He glanced at Ty.

"Seems sound to me," Ty said. "Fair to the kid and to the witness."

Elizabeth stepped closer to her husband. Ty heard her speak to him in a low tone of voice. "He's right, Wade."

Major Lange stepped back as though giving the lawman room to consider a new idea.

Rogers nodded slowly. A man sure of himself, he was not one to alter his thinking easily. He respected Ty, though, and his wife's advice could not be ignored. The more he considered the plan suggested by Major Lange, the more vigorously he nodded.

Ty saw the lawman reach to his suit coat. Hesitating for a moment, he grasped the badge and pulled it off his lapel.

Chapter Eight

"I told you! Damned, if I didn't tell you! I never killed nobody!"

From the security of a railroad car with shades drawn, the unseen witness had testified to the innocence of every man or boy on the railroad platform that day—including the kid, Smitty, George, and Dean. The murderer she had seen in Denver was not among them. Of that, she was certain. Once the U.S. marshal confirmed her testimony, the night hawk of the Circle L Ranch was freed, his few possessions and his sheathed Green River knife returned to him.

Ty looked on as the federal lawman consulted Rogers. The marshal picked up box lunches from Bertha's café. Within the hour the locomotive built a head of steam under billowing black coal smoke, and mother and daughter departed, unseen by passengers and onlookers in Coalton.

"I told you!" the kid shouted to the heavens. "Didn't I tell you?"

Ty saw Rose and Sharon abruptly turn their backs on the kid. Dropping their mallets, they headed for the Pullman cars in long strides, coiffed heads thrust back, powdered noses upturned as though escaping a foul odor.

Preoccupied with events of the moment, the kid was

blithely unaware of their sudden departure, much less their obvious distaste for him. Intent on celebrating his brush with a hangman's rope, the kid rushed to the Comet.

At the bar he claimed to be eighteen and demanded the genuine article—ale instead of sarsaparilla. He called for one mug of brew chased by a shot of rye whiskey, Old Overholt, if you please, as if his declaration of innocence had somehow promoted him to manhood. His urgent request for a celebratory boiler-maker was quietly denied by Ray Owens.

"Hell, I'm old enough," the kid protested, his face flushed in anger. "I can pay. I've got money."

Ray did not bother to argue. For this barkeep, who had heard it all and seen most of it, the subject was neither under discussion nor up for debate. His reply was the dismissive wave of a hand in the general direction of the saloon's batwing doors.

The kid cursed. "There's plenty of other saloons in this burg!"

"Go find one," Ray said.

The kid stormed out, paused, and angled toward the players in the vacant lot. On the croquet course he saw Ty standing aside while Major Lange whacked a ball around with six other players.

In his rôle of host, Lange had invited townsfolk to join in. He offered instructions. A few had played croquet, and others had seen the game played in city parks—"billiards on grass", as it was commonly known. By any name, locals eagerly tried their hand at executing unique strategies involved in "mallets of forethought".

Ty saw the kid crossing the street. He joined them, still gloating over the incontrovertible proof of innocence that had freed him. *I told you!* Eyeing the croquet match for a

time, he let out a boast like the hiss of steam from a locomotive.

"Hell, I could beat anyone at this damned game," he
said.

Major Lange handed him ˙a mallet and ball. "Be my
guest," he said, and stepped back.

Bearing down with mighty swings, the kid played in a
haphazard, heavy-handed manner. When his ball rolled into
a clump of pear cactus, he gingerly picked it up and placed
it on bare ground, positioned for a sure shot to the next
wicket.

"Play the lie," Major Lange said, informing him the
rules did not permit such manipulations. "Play your ball as
you find it."

The kid ignored him. He left the ball where it was while
impatiently awaiting his turn. Even though he openly
cheated as play progressed, he was not only faced with de-
feat by the other players, he was trounced when Major
Lange closed in and executed a send.

The kid swore as his green ball rolled to the far side of
the course, setting up Lange's impending victory. After
that, he exhibited little patience for the game. Observers
laughed when he swung hard and missed the ball altogether. In another wild, misguided swing, he swore at a
second clean miss. Raising the mallet overhead, then, the
kid slammed it to the ground. The handle broke off from
the head with a loud *crack*.

Uttering profanities, the kid dropped the handle and
spun away. He was intent on leaving this scene of civilized
madness until the ramrod's voice stopped him in his tracks.

"Pay the man for that busted mallet."

Onlookers fell silent as the kid faced him. No one spoke
until Major Lange stepped forward.

"That won't be necessary, Ty," he said. "It's a small matter."

"No, the night hawk can pay for his damages," Ty insisted. He added pointedly: "Or he can work them off."

The kid's jaw tightened. "I ain't doing no chores for a man who keeps servants."

"Then pay cash," Ty said. "One way or another, you're not leaving here without settling your debt." He glanced at Lange. "Two dollars ought to square things. That about right?"

Eyes downcast, Major Lange offered no opinion.

For a long moment the kid seemed ready to defy the ramrod. Then he dug into a trouser pocket and pulled out assorted greenbacks. Holding two $1 bills in his hand, he raised his arm and let them flutter to the ground. He turned and walked away.

Ty watched the kid cross the street, headed for the saloon district. "Still needs a lesson or two in manners, doesn't he?"

"The youngster's had a bad time of it," Lange said.

Ty bent down and picked up the greenbacks. "That's no excuse in my book," he said, straightening up.

Lange shook his head when Ty offered the money to him. Ty insisted, and finally Lange relented. Accepting the two ones, he reluctantly pocketed the money.

Ty did not see the kid again until after nightfall. Standing at the bar of the Comet with Smitty, he saw him stagger in, lurching as though crossing the deck of a ship tossed by high seas. Joining them, the kid grinned crazily and grabbed the raised edge of the bar for support.

"Where have you been?" Smitty demanded.

The kid answered with a defiant shrug. "Hell, I don't 'member."

Ty eyed him. "Be ready to ride, come morning."

Replying in combative, yet unintelligible sounds, the kid slurred his defiant refusal.

Ty leaned closer to him. He repeated his order over the din of other voices in the saloon. "If you aim to stick on the Circle L, you'll ride out in the morning with Smitty and me. Corny has chores waiting for you. . . ."

Raging, the kid reared back and took a swing at Ty. The roundhouse punch was as reckless as it was unexpected, and connected with full force. Rocked back, Ty's knees buckled. He sank to the floor and fell back with a roaring sound filling his ears. The kid stood over him as he stared up at the fleur-de-lis pattern in the pressed tin ceiling.

"I've been waiting a long time to do that, you son-of-a-bitch!" he shouted. Swaying, he broke away and staggered out of the saloon.

Even though conscious, Ty was uncertain where he was or what had happened to him. He struggled as Smitty helped him to his feet and brushed sawdust from his clothing. The loud roar crashed around him like a waterfall. Saloon patrons stared, shocked at the sight of Smitty guiding the semi-conscious man to a chair at the nearest table. Ty slumped into it, head lolling.

"What . . . what happened?"

"The night hawk sucker-punched you," Smitty replied. "Damn! You all right, Ty? Ray! Ray! Bring some water, will you? And a bar towel. Bring a wet bar towel."

In the morning Ty awoke in a rooming house with a headache and blurred vision. The waterfall roar had subsided. His jaw ached. He gingerly probed a walnut-sized knot there. Over the years he had stepped into a bar fight or two, but he had never been tagged like that before. Except for a blur of bizarre images and fractured memories, he recalled little of what had transpired last night. He knew the kid had hit him with a looping punch that came out of nowhere. He knew Smitty had lent assistance to get him off the floor and into a chair. But he did not remember coming here.

Now he did not know why Sheriff Rogers and Smitty stood at the foot of his bed in the rooming house, either. Hats in hand, they were glum, as though facing a funeral.

Feeling disconnected from reality, Ty listened intently as Smitty and Sheriff Rogers filled in the blanks. The lawman began with the fact that Major Lange had been reported missing before dawn.

"Missing?" Ty repeated as though the word made no sense to him.

Sheriff Rogers said: "Rose and Sharon waited half the night in their Pullman car for him."

When Major Lange did not arrive as expected, Rogers went on, the sisters searched the other three private cars. Outside, they walked between stacks of ties, coal bins, and investigated the immediate area around the siding. No sign of him, anywhere. They dared not venture into the saloon district, and sent Edgar to look for him. The manservant came back in an hour, empty-handed.

Rose and Sharon waited for Major Lange as long as they could bear it. They believed he was in town, somewhere, and would eventually return to their cars. Yet as time wore on, a grim realization that something had happened to him was undeniable.

They ventured far enough away from the safety of their rail car to notify a night deputy. The deputy had not seen Lange. He knew the man by sight, and shared their concern. He agreed Lange had to be in Coalton or somewhere nearby. Back alleys and thickets were searched by the light of lanterns.

The body was not found until daybreak when a croquet mallet was discovered floating in the greenish waters of a thermal spring. 100 yards away from town, the site drew a crowd as word spread.

Morning air sent wisps of steam rising from the surface like spirits from the netherworld. Voices hushed, more townsfolk congregated in a ghostly scene. Light from the rising sun illuminated the remains of a man submerged in a turquoise pool. The corpse was magnified, weirdly distorted as though viewed through a fluid lens.

Dragged out of the spring, the body steamed in the chilled air of morning. Sheriff Rogers readily identified the dead man from his clothing, stature, and trimmed Vandyke beard. Cause of death was no accident. Rogers noted circular imprints on the forehead of the corpse, dark bruises that matched the head of a croquet mallet in diameter.

Major Lange murdered.

Ty stared at Sheriff Rogers. Now he understood his glum demeanor, the reason his jaw was set in an expression of grim determination. Rose and Sharon had reported seeing the kid stagger past their car last evening. The sisters heard shouts. An argument erupted, and they overheard the kid demand $2.

You rich bastard! What do you care about two dollars? Give me my money! Give it back!

By then, Sheriff Rogers had heard enough. The charge of murder was lodged in absentia against the kid, a judicial writ in the form of an arrest warrant. Via telegraph, Rogers requested a circuit judge be dispatched to Coalton, *pronto*.

Now, to find the fugitive. A methodical search of brush by the creek and entry into every building and shed in town confirmed initial suspicions. The kid was gone.

Ty sat up in bed, wincing with the effort. His head throbbed with his every move.

Smitty anticipated the next question. "I went to Jim's livery barn, Ty. The roan's not there."

Rogers considered the implications of the ranch hand's remark. "Where do you think he went?"

"Dunno," Smitty replied. "But I can tell you he won't get there any time soon."

"Why do you say that?" the lawman asked.

"He's riding the slowest horse in the Circle L string," he replied.

Ty thought about that. "He might head for the home place."

"The Circle L?" Rogers asked. "Why would he do that?"

"Corny has no way of knowing he's on the run," Ty replied. "The kid can load up on food from the pantry, and saddle a fresh horse from the barn. That gets him a long lead on a posse."

"Speaking of a posse," Rogers said, turning to Smitty, "I could use a hand. I know you and that kid were pards, but are you willing to pin on a badge and ride after him with me?"

Smitty jerked his thumb toward Ty. "I work for him."

"Wear the badge," Rogers said, "and you'll be working for me. I'm asking, Smitty. Can you take the oath and do your duty?"

Smitty gave the question his usual thoughtful consideration before answering. "Yes, sir, I reckon I can."

"You're sure?" Rogers asked, and repeated: "He was your pard."

"No saddle pard of mine would kill a man over two dollars," Smitty said. "We need to bring the kid in."

"All right," Rogers said. "We'll ride. Draw rations from the mercantile. You'll be paid by the county . . . three dollars a day."

Ty's vision had cleared, but his head throbbed when he leaned down to reach for his boots on the floor beside the bed. "Count me in, Sheriff."

"You're in no shape to make a long ride," Rogers said.

"I'm in no shape to lay here flat on my back," Ty countered, "while you and my top hand wander through the countryside."

Rogers gazed at him, and shook his head. "Stay here, Ty."

The ramrod's beard-stubbled jaw twisted in pain when he pulled on one boot and then the other. He eyed Sheriff Rogers.

"One thing I'm not clear on, Wade."

"What's that?"

"How you aim to stop me from riding to the ranch," Ty replied.

"Yeah, the night hawk was here."

The sheriff's question was answered by Corny after the three riders cantered into the yard at Circle L headquarters. Dismounting, Ty, Smitty, and Sheriff Rogers led their horses to the water trough.

"The night hawk's been here and gone," the ranch cook went on. "Damned near rode that ol' roan into the ground. I grained him and turned him out to pasture myself. The night hawk tried to throw a saddle on that wild mare, but he couldn't catch her." Corny drew a breath. "I caught him leading your chestnut gelding out of the barn, Ty. You know the one?"

"Blaze face?" Ty asked.

"That's the one," Corny said. "The night hawk rode out on him. Claimed he had your permission to take any mount from the remuda. Said something about running down a coal prospector trespassing on Circle L range. Any truth to it?"

Ty shook his head. "Not much."

"I had a feeling he was lying," Corny said with a scowl. "Can't trust a kid who eats like swine and talks like Satan."

"He's desperate," Sheriff Rogers said.

"How's that?" Corny asked.

It was one thing to pick a liar out of a crowd, but the ranch cook was flabbergasted when Rogers recounted recent events in Coalton. Corny was amazed to learn the kid was on the run, that he had been charged with the murder of Major Lange.

Corny said: "I turned my back on him a time or two. Reckon I'm lucky he didn't bash my brains in, too." He lamented: "Wish I could tell you gents where he ran off to."

Smitty added: "Wish I'd never taught him to saddle a horse."

Sheriff Rogers said: "We'll get him."

"I'll rustle up supper for you, gents, quick-like," Corny said. Turning, he spoke over his shoulder as he headed toward the cook shack. "You'll need a hot meal before you hit the saddles."

Ty looked around the place after he tended his horse and turned him into a fenced pasture. He felt like a stranger in his own domain. Wind-blown weeds were tangled on the south side of the barn. He saw a grain spill that had not been cleaned up, a busted hay bale near the barn door, and stock troughs less than half full. The door to the ranch house stood open, an oversight that bothered him.

Angling across the yard, Ty mounted the steps and

crossed the verandah to the doorway. He stepped inside. The interior was too neat and too clean for a man's ease of comfort. The place on the desktop occupied by the photographic portrait of a young woman with her baby was bare, too.

Something else was out of place. Ty looked around and took note of an act of thievery. His Winchester repeater was gone.

A single set of tracks left by a shod horse was not difficult to follow over dry prairie in broad daylight. Ty felt certain the kid was riding the horse that had left this trail. He seemed to be backtracking steers, probably headed for the wetland near the coal seam. Ty figured he had overheard enough discussion about it to know he could simply follow the broad trail left by fourteen outlaw steers to his destination.

Destination. As he rode, Ty thought about the end of the trail. He wondered if the kid meant to hide out, for a while at least, in the abandoned cabin. Where he would go from there, Ty could only guess. Maybe the kid himself did not know. Like a pup out the door, maybe he was running for the sheer exhilaration of unfettered freedom.

At nightfall, they halted by a seep and made a cold camp. After refilling canteens, they grained and tended their horses. They ate a supper of baked beans, greasy biscuits, sardines, and peach halves from tins. Ty's jaw ached as he chewed. The knot was sore to the touch, but he was no longer dizzy or disoriented. He knew all too well what had to be done when the kid was run to ground.

"My rifle wasn't in the ranch house where I left it," Ty said now.

Rogers dragged a hand through his beard. "You figure the kid stole it?"

Ty nodded. "Seems so."

"Does he know how to use it?"

Smitty spoke up. "I borrowed Ty's rifle for some target shooting a while back. The kid tagged along and squeezed off a few rounds."

The lawman thought about that. "We'll take him after nightfall. No sense in giving him any easy shots when we close in."

With that Rogers ate heartily. Afterward he reclined on a sougan and queried Ty about Major Lange. For himself, the lawman had spoken to him on numerous occasions and, of course, had been invited to the infamous dinner in the Pullman car, but he did not know the man well enough to be conversant about him.

Ty gazed at a star-filled sky. Memories were like distant spheres in the heavens, he thought, bright and distinct, yet at once unknown. He would never forget the first time he laid eyes on Major Gregory Lange. Striding to Ty's table in the dining room of the Coalton House, the diminutive man had brought news of his mother's death. Ty had declared him mad.

Later, Lange had spoken tersely of his upbringing. Educated in the classics by tutors, he had been lonely as a child, particularly after the passing of his father. He spoke little of his mother, other than citing the fact that she had held off the Grim Reaper far longer than anyone had believed possible. Ty remembered that much from Lange's reminiscences.

He knew Major Lange to be a man of wealth and generosity, a rare combination of traits in a man. In Ty's experience, limited as it was, the rich were ruthless, heartless, and lived the diametrical opposite of a selfless life. The rich grabbed and got. They insisted on living like lords, convinced accumulated riches secured passage through pearly gates, and the greater their wealth, the louder heavenly hosts trumpeted their entry into the gold-paved avenues of heaven.

The relationship between Ty and Major Lange was not unique in the annals of 19th Century ranching. A business built exclusively on trust, the ranch operated by virtue of what amounted to a long-distance handshake. What was unique was the unparalleled prosperity of the Circle L. Vast cattle outfits that had made stockmen wealthy from Wyoming to Montana had gone bust after winter die-ups. To the north, blizzards had claimed entire herds while livestock wearing the Circle L brand flourished. Back East beef prices sky-rocketed.

Major Lange had awarded his ramrod full credit for the stellar success of the Circle L Ranch, but Ty knew better. According to the old saw, success in the cattle business was determined fifty percent by weather, fifty percent by terrain, and fifty percent by dumb luck.

Smitty gave voice to the question that lurked in the back of Ty's mind. "What's gonna happen to the Circle L?"

"Reckon some gent will buy it from the Lange estate," Ty replied, "and run cattle on it."

Sheriff Rogers looked on with interest.

"Whoever the buyer is," Smitty said, "if he has a lick of sense, he'll hire you to ramrod the outfit."

"I'll drink to that," Rogers said.

Ty shrugged. "Save your liquor, gents. New owner usually means new foreman." Eager to change the subject, he turned to Sheriff Rogers. "Are the two ladies and their servants still bunking in those private cars?"

Rogers nodded. "They might as well nail their shoes to the floorboards."

Smitty asked: "Why do you say that?"

"They're material witnesses," Rogers answered.

"What does that mean?" Smitty asked.

"It means they are obligated to remain in Coalton," he replied, "until the circuit judge gets there for the preliminary hearing. From then on the judge calls the shots."

"Reckon the sisters were mighty happy to hear that," Smitty said, deadpan.

"They aim to see the kid brought to justice," Rogers said. "Rose told me the sooner the better. After he's convicted, the sisters will take Lange's remains back to Maryland."

When dawn broke, the three of them were in the saddle again. Wade Rogers, a big man on a big horse, did not utter a word of complaint, but he was clearly uncomfortable sitting a saddle for so many consecutive hours. Even with stops to rest man and beast, Ty saw the lawman grimace with every step, pained by legs chafed from the friction of the repetitive motion of his mount.

Rogers was not completely unprepared for this misery. Dismounting frequently along the way, he dropped his trousers and liberally applied horse liniment to the inflamed skin of his inner thighs. The treatment brought relief for a while.

At midday Ty drew rein. He stood in the stirrups and pointed to a stretch of prairie ahead. A thin cloud of dust drifted skyward. Rogers and Smitty halted beside him. Moments later a herd of mustangs swung into view.

Ty saw Domino in the lead, moving fast. The big stallion veered away, galloping with tail up, mane flying. Reins held taut, Smitty and Rogers stared after the fleeing herd. Ty grinned, knowing he was witness to a sight rarely seen on the prairie in this day and age.

Smitty turned to Ty. "You missed your chance to put a bullet through that thieving stallion."

The joke was not lost on the ramrod. "Let him run. Let him steal all of the Circle L mares he wants."

Smitty grinned. He turned to Rogers and filled him in on the background of their repartée.

Ty saw Smitty pull off his hat and wipe his brow with a bandanna. The ranch hand discretely turned away and wiped his eyes. At times sadness and merriment were closely linked, Ty thought, and sometimes laughter brought tears. These were shed in memory of Bill Connors.

They made a hard ride. In the gathering darkness the three riders drew in sight of the rise overlooking the marsh and the homesteader's cabin. Ty smelled sage-tinged smoke. He lifted his hand in a silent signal. He expected the kid to be there, but he would not be certain until he looked over the crest of that rise to see for himself.

Dismounting, Ty pulled off his spurs. Rowels jingled briefly as he put them on his saddle horn. Rogers and Smitty followed his example. Then they bent low as they made their way to the top of the rise. Dropping to all fours near the crest, they crawled around cactus and sage until the ruined cabin came into view below. A campfire blazed down there.

Ty's gaze was drawn to flames in front of that tumble-down cabin. By that firelight he saw a Circle L saddle mount—the chestnut gelding—hobbled in the grass nearby. Presently Rogers whispered urgently as he pointed to the far side of the cabin: "There he is."

Ty looked where he pointed and saw the kid move out of the deep shadows beside the cabin. Dragging branches from a dried sagebrush, he pitched one into the flames. Smoke billowed until the fire flared up, the blaze highlighting a trail-worn kid. Disheveled, he wore duds purchased for him in the Coalton Mercantile, dirty now. Ty watched him. If the kid meant to hide, he thought, he was doing a poor job of it.

At Rogers's signal, they backed away and crawled down the slope where they could stand without being seen. Rogers looked back the way they had come. He spoke in a low tone. "We'd better take him now," Rogers said, "before a horse whickers or something else tips him off." The lawman motioned toward the homesteader's claim. "Spread out and move fast. Campfire flames will dazzle his eyes. If we close in from three sides and rush him, he won't know what hit him. If he goes for his knife or takes up Ty's rifle. . . ."

Ty saw the lawman's gaze shift to Smitty.

"Kill him if you have to," Rogers said.

Smitty nodded once.

The lawman's final word of advice was sobering. In the dim light of evening the three of them gazed at one another while a long moment of silence passed between them.

Ty wondered if Smitty could level his gun, aim, and pull the trigger with the kid in his sights. Could he kill the kid he had befriended? In truth, Ty harbored the same question about his own resolve. He had never shot a man before, much less a kid. Whether he could now or not, this was not the time for discussion. Without exchanging another word, he knew each of them was keenly aware of standing on the edge of an abyss—three men, armed, ready to leap into violence.

Ty checked the loads in his revolver while Smitty jacked a round into the chamber of his rifle. Rogers drew his Peacemaker. Upon his hand-signaled directions, then, they went their separate ways.

Topping the rise, Ty used the campfire as a beacon. He moved swiftly over the crest and headed downslope toward the cabin. He was aware of grass and weeds crunching underfoot, and pear cactus kicked by the toes of his boots. His heart pounded. The impact of each step seemed loud in those moments, even though he knew the sounds were muffled by distance or drowned out by the crackling campfire. He glimpsed a shadowy figure to his right. Downrange, Rogers lumbered toward the blazing campfire. Smitty, the third prong in their fast-moving attack, loped along as they closed in.

"Hands up!" Rogers called out.

The kid was startled by the shouted command. He had been kneeling by the fire, and now he straightened and at once staggered back, his left boot tangling with the right. Arms waving furiously, he nearly went down.

Rogers shouted again: "Hands up! Hands up, or we'll shoot!"

The kid caught his balance. He meekly surrendered, raising both arms straight up as he faced the guns and pounding footfalls of men running toward him. Shocked, he recognized them in the pale light only when they drew closer.

"What the hell . . . ?"

"Drop your knife!" Rogers shouted, breathless from his exertion. "Drop it!"

The kid did as he was told. Pulling the knife from its sheath, he let it fall into the dirt at his feet. His gaze swung to Ty.

"I don't know what Corny told you," the kid said, "but I aimed to bring your horse back to the barn. That's the truth. I ain't no horse thief. I was hunting that prospector, the one trespassing on Circle L range. I figured if I brung

142

him in, you'd let go of hard feelings toward me. You know, for punching you in the face like I done. That's the truth."

"That's a cock-and-bull story," Rogers countered, "if I ever heard one."

The kid faced him. "I'm telling you the truth!"

While they glowered at one another, Ty asked: "Where's my rifle, son?"

The kid jerked a thumb toward the cabin. "Figured I might need it to run off trespassers. . . ." His voice trailed off.

Ty turned and saw his Winchester propped against a log wall. Over decades the logs had partially collapsed under the weight of snow, and leaned away from the shove of winter winds. On the ground nearby, Ty saw the Circle L saddle and bridle where the kid had left them.

"That's the honest truth," the kid said again.

"You and the truth," Rogers said, still breathing hard, "don't run too close."

Holstering his revolver, Ty moved past him and took the rifle in hand.

"Hell, I'm sorry I hit you, Ty," the kid said to him. He held his right hand out. "I hurt my damned hand. It's all swolled up. Might have busted a knuckle."

"Well, ain't that just sorrowful sad," Smitty said.

The kid spun around and faced him. "I know I done wrong, Smitty. I was drunk."

"Drunk or sober," Smitty said, "you sucker-punched the man who gave you work, the man who put clothes on your back, the man who set food before you. You were skinny as a rail when the ramrod brought you to the home ranch like a starving pup. . . ."

"Smitty, I know all that," he broke in. "That's why I'm telling you. . . ."

Rogers said: "Telling us what?"

"I told you I aimed to make good by catching that prospector trespassing on Circle L range," he said. "He was in a saloon where I was drinking with a bunch of coal miners. When he left, I followed him to the livery. I figured if I caught him red-handed on Circle L land, you wouldn't hold no hard feelings against me. . . ."

"That isn't why we're here," Rogers broke in, "and you know it."

"Know what?" the kid asked.

"You clubbed Major Lange with a croquet mallet," Rogers said, "and then you rolled his body into that hot spring."

By the light of dancing flames, Ty saw the kid's jaw drop.

"Huh?" he said.

"Don't dummy up on me," Rogers said.

"I don't know what the hell you're talking about," the kid said. "You're saying . . . you're saying . . . that Lange dude . . . he's dead?"

"You know damn' well he is," Rogers said. "If he wasn't killed when you brained him, he drowned in the boiling water when you dragged him to that spring and rolled him into it. Either way, it was a hell of a way to die."

"I never. . . ."

"You killed the man who saved your neck from a hangman's rope," Rogers interrupted. "Killed him over two dollars."

The kid shook his head. "Sheriff, I never killed nobody. I didn't have no idea he was dead. . . ."

"You argued with him," Rogers countered. "Witnesses heard you."

"I told you I was drunk," the kid repeated. "I wanted

144

more liquor. That was all I could think about. Lange handed over my two dollars. I never seen him after that. I sure as hell never killed him."

"The truth will come out," Rogers said, "after the judge and jury hear the whole story."

The kid stared at him. "What do you mean by that?"

"I figure there's a good reason that witness from Denver didn't pick you out of a crowd," Rogers said.

"What reason?"

"You look a sight different than the last time she saw you," he said. "Hair cropped short, big hat, neckerchief, cowhand duds . . . you look like a trail hand, not some runaway kid begging hand-to-mouth in a depot."

"I never killed nobody," he said dully.

"You just keep singing that sorry song," Rogers said. "Sing it all the way to my jail." The lawman turned away from him. "Smitty, get the irons out of my saddlebags, and we'll cinch up the prisoner. Ty, if you'll bring up the horses, we'll make camp here."

Ty nodded. As he turned away, he heard an anguished cry. He looked back. By firelight he saw the kid cast a pleading look at him. Caked with prairie dust, his lean face was smudged with soot from campfire ashes.

Ty walked away, thinking about the child-like cry and those fire-lit eyes. He made no claim to prescience, but at that moment he sensed he would never forget the plaintive tone in the kid's voice or that look in his face. The anguished cry was an expression of raw fear, a wordless plea for his life.

"I knew that kid was no good, Tyler. I just knew it."

Seated by the café window looking out on Front Street, Ty ate beef stew and a buttered soda biscuit while Bertha stood over him and held forth. Late in the morning, he was the sole customer, her only audience.

"He hadn't been in Coalton but two days when he tried to jimmy my back door with his knife blade," she said. "That was after I gave him supper from leftovers out the same door. Was that good enough for him? No, it wasn't. He came back in the night for more, probably aiming to steal anything he could get his hands on." Bertha's ample breasts heaved when she drew a deep breath. "He's worse than your run-of-the-mill thief, Tyler, ten times worse."

The door to the café opened. Ty saw Smitty enter. Spurs jingled when the ranch hand crossed the café to the table by the window. Pulling off his hat, he greeted Bertha before turning to Ty.

"Sheriff's on his way to settle up," Smitty said.

"After he pays us," Ty said, "we'll ride."

Smitty gazed out the window. "I'm plumb ready."

Ty nodded in agreement. "Reckon I've had enough of Stink Water Junction to last me a spell, too."

Bertha asked: "Where do I get in line?"

Smitty turned to her. "In line to get out of this burg?"

"No," she said. "You said the sheriff's paying you. Where do I get in line for free money?"

"Wasn't hardly free," Smitty said.

Ty explained: "The county pays posse men three dollars a day."

Bertha gave the matter some thought. "I should have rode with you boys."

Smitty eyed her, a smile wrinkling laugh lines in his weathered face. The notion of a woman riding with a posse was novel. "Bertha, what would you have done when we caught up with the fugitive?"

"I'd have found the nearest tree," she replied, "and the shortest rope."

Ty grinned. "Next time, you ride with the lawman. I'll stick to easy work . . . such as roping yearlings and herding cattle."

"Fair enough," she said.

Smitty pointed to Ty's bowl. "Reckon I'll have me a helping of that there stew, ma'am. Ladle in plenty of it, if you would."

"With a biscuit . . . ," she asked, "fresh baked this morning?"

"Yes, ma'am," he said. "Make that two. Two biscuits slathered with that apple butter you put up every fall."

Ty was working on his second cup of coffee when he heard the door open. He turned in the chair. Sheriff Rogers stepped into the café and held the door open for his wife.

Ty watched Elizabeth Rogers enter. Well dressed as usual, she wore a long, serge outfit, caped, with decorative cuffs, white gloves, and a modest hat trailing a single red ribbon. She lifted her hand in greetings to Ty and Smitty, and strode toward the kitchen.

Ty remembered that the sheriff's wife worked with Bertha to schedule meals for prisoners in the jail. *This particular prisoner,* he thought, *would receive free food from the establishment he had attempted to burglarize.*

Rogers came to the table and drew out his wallet. He counted out greenbacks in the amount of $12 per deputy. Paying Ty and Smitty, he thanked both men for their service to Coalton County. Then he turned to Ty.

"The kid asked if you were still in town," Rogers said. "Says he wants to see you."

Ty looked at the lawman in surprise.

"If you don't want to talk to him," Rogers went on, "I'll

tell him you and Smitty already rode out."

Ty pushed his chair back and stood. "No, I'll see him. I've got some time while Smitty chows down on stew, or whatever it is."

On the way to the cell-block next to the sheriff's office, the lawman spoke confidentially to Ty. "Seems like I'm always asking you for favors. Now I've got another one."

"What is it?" Ty asked.

"If the kid confesses to the murder of Major Lange," he replied as they followed the plank walk, "write down what he says. Write it down word for word. Put today's date on it, and sign it. When the judge gets here, we'll use it for evidence."

Mystified, Ty eyed him. "What makes you think he'll confess to me . . . or to anyone?"

"He's acting strange," Rogers replied.

"Strange?"

"Like something's weighing on him," the lawman said. "He looks up to you. It's a long shot, but I figured when he sees you, maybe he'll unburden himself. You know . . . get it off his chest."

Ty corrected him. "The kid doesn't look up to me. I've been a little rough on him out at the ranch. Most of the time, we don't get along."

"I know you see it that way," Rogers conceded, "but I figure the kid's looking at things from a different angle."

"What are you driving at?"

"If you've ridden him hard," he replied, "that just shows him you give a damn. Maybe nobody has ever handed him that much respect before."

Ty had to admit he had never viewed their contentious relationship in this light. He considered it now, remembering their conflicts. From time to time he had seen the kid fly into a red rage, mad enough to kill. For himself, from time to time Ty had been mad enough to run him off the place.

"If I'm right," the lawman concluded, "the kid figures he can talk to you, straight out. Maybe he'll confess."

Ty left his revolver with Rogers and went into the cellblock. He understood what the sheriff had meant by "acting strange" when he found the kid huddled on the narrow bunk with his knees drawn up. Instead of ranting and raving, cussing and threatening, he was lethargic. Here in the stark confines of the jail cell, the kid's spirit seemed broken. He did not acknowledge Ty's presence until the ramrod spoke to him.

"Night hawk."

The kid stirred. He swung his feet down and sat up. He left the bunk and slowly moved to the barred door, head bowed. Ty noted he had bathed, but his clothing was not clean. Barefoot and bare headed, the kid stood before him, eyes downcast.

Ty found himself recalling the first time they met. Sheriff Rogers had brought him into the Comet and introduced him. Ty remembered the shabby, patched clothing the kid had worn that day—boots held together with wire, a length of cotton rope for a belt, a battered hat two sizes too large. He remembered high, pointed cheek bones in a lean, sunburned face, and he remembered those gray, coyote eyes. Now when the kid spoke, his voice was barely audible.

"The sisters did it."

Chapter Nine

Speechless for the moment, Ty stared at him. *Sisters?*

At first he thought the kid had mumbled something else. *Scissors did it?*

"The sisters did it."

When the kid repeated his accusation, wild thoughts stampeded through Ty's mind. "What . . . what are you trying to say?"

"You heard me."

Ty cleared his throat. "Are you telling me . . . Rose and Sharon . . . are you telling me . . . they killed Major Lange?"

"Nobody's gonna believe me," the kid answered in a monotone. "I know that. You don't even believe me. Do you?"

Ty had to admit the kid was right about that. He did not believe him. How could he? The whole idea was preposterous. Regardless of spats and arguments, for those two women to have clubbed Major Lange and dragged his body to the thermal spring where they rolled him into the boiling waters was not just improbable, it was impossible.

"Everybody in this stinking town wants to see me hang," the kid went on. "There ain't no stopping it. Some hanging judge is gonna say I killed that dude, Lange. Sheriff Rogers, he'll buy a brand new suit so's he'll look good for my lynching. Folks around here will call it justice when my neck snaps."

Ty was taken aback by his nonchalance. The kid's matter-of-fact prediction of a great wrong was not driven by fear now so much as it was by deep sorrow. Ty saw that in his demeanor. He saw it in a slackening of his shoulders and a resignation in his eyes. Swaying, the kid wavered as though he might fall. He grasped the bars, and caught his balance. His gaze came to rest on Ty.

"Hell, I never should have punched you like I done," he said. "Never should have cussed you, neither. I was drunk. . . ."

While he spoke, Ty reflected on Sheriff Rogers's insights into the nature of this kid. Clearly the lawman had altered his assessment of him, a view that had changed a great deal from the time they met to the day of his arrest.

"Sometimes I get so damned mad. . . ."

Ty listened as the kid's voice trailed off again.

Then he went on: "There's been times when I was so mad at you. . . ."

Ty finished the sentence: "So mad you wanted to kill me?"

The kid shook his head. "Not that mad."

"The last time you were locked up in this cell," Ty reminded him, "you threatened to kill a man someday. You shouted threats at everyone in earshot on this end of Front Street."

The kid eyed him. "But I never killed nobody."

"Ask the sheriff about that," Ty said.

"What are you driving at?"

"He'll tell you most folks around here figure you killed

Major Lange," Ty said. "Some believe you killed a girl in Denver and got away with it."

"Hell, I know that," he said. "That's why I wanted to talk to you. You're the only one who ever listened worth a damn. I want you to know the truth."

Ty watched as the kid drew a breath, his eyes narrowing.

"Them two sisters killed him," he went on. "After I hang, that will still be the truth."

Ty asked: "How do you know it is?"

"Can't be no other way," the kid retorted. "It just can't."

"Why do you say that?"

"I know I didn't kill him," the kid said. "So who else in this burg could have? Has to be Rose and Sharon. That's why they're pointing the finger at me. They don't want folks thinking about blaming anybody else."

Ty said: "The sisters claim you and Lange argued."

"I ain't denying that part of it," he said.

"They say you argued over two dollars," Ty went on. "And you threatened him."

"That's about half true," he said.

"Which half?" Ty asked.

"I never threatened him," the kid said.

"You sure about that?"

"I told you," the kid said. "I was drunk. All I could think about was getting another drink. The only way I could get money for liquor was to take it from that dude, Lange. I figured two dollars in his pocket belonged to me. I told him to hand it over, and he did. I never pulled my knife on him."

The kid paused. "A jug of that eye-talian wine was the cheapest liquor I could get. I bought it in a saloon full of miners. That's where I seen that coal prospector. I kept an eye on him. Followed him to the livery. When he rode out

152

of town, I tracked him. That old plug couldn't keep up. With nobody out there but me and the coyotes, I drank wine until I passed out. Don't you see? I couldn't have killed Lange."

Ty paused. "I still don't savvy why you figure the sisters killed Major Lange."

The kid replied without hesitation. "He told Rose he wasn't gonna marry her. Said she wasn't gonna get any of his money, either."

"You heard him say that?" Ty asked.

"Hell, yes," the kid said. "After I got my two dollars back from the dude, I was standing outside their parlor car. I heard Lange. He and Rose were arguing. He said it was a bad mistake to bring her to Colorado. Said they were going back to Maryland, *pronto*, and he was taking the sisters straight back to their mother. Rose screamed at him. They fought like fury."

"Did anyone else hear them?"

He shrugged. "Maybe the servants heard that cater-wauling. I dunno. It don't matter. Nobody's gonna believe me."

Ty watched the kid turn away. He figured that last remark was not born of self-pity so much as it was a statement of incontrovertible fact in his mind. The kid moved to the back corner of his cell and slumped down on the bunk.

Ty thought back to his capture at the abandoned home-steader's cabin. He remembered the sound of the kid's voice when he had cried out in despair, uttering a child's anguished plea. The kid knew Sheriff Rogers would keep him in wrist and leg irons and deliver him from that camp-site to a cell in the Coalton jail. The inevitability of confinement was more than he could bear.

At the time of their confrontation, Ty had felt great relief when the kid surrendered quickly. Beyond demonstrating he was more boy than man, it was a measure of good fortune. Ty had not wanted to shoot anyone, least of all a youngster crying and scared half out of his wits. He thought about that as he turned away to leave the cell-block.

"Mister Johnson."

Ty stopped. He turned back, eyeing the kid. It was the first time in a long while he had addressed him respectfully.

"That photographic pitcher I seen."

Ty moved closer to the bars. "Pitcher?"

"In the ranch house I seen that pitcher portrait you was holding," he said. "A mother and her baby."

Ty nodded. "What about it?"

The kid eyed him, clearly searching for the right words to frame his question. "Who's in that pitcher?"

"My wife, Sarah, and our son, Will," Ty replied.

"I never knew you had a wife and son," the kid said.

"I don't," Ty said.

"What do you mean?"

"They died in a flu outbreak," Ty said. He added: "A long time ago."

The kid stared at him, for once at a loss for words.

When it was obvious neither of them had more to say, Ty turned away. He left the cell-block. Outside, he stood on the plank walk, watching and listening.

Unlike the quietude of ranch life, the town was vibrant, alive with the sounds of horse-drawn vehicles and the voices of passers-by. Heels of boots and shoes resounded on the plank walk like drumbeats. The rhythmic *clip-clop* of draft horses and the musical *clinking* of harness chains reached him when freight wagons rolled past. The rigs were followed by an overland coach loaded with passengers.

Down the street the U.P. platform stood empty. *Not*

154

everyone traveled by train or shipped goods by rail these days, he thought.

Amid the traffic sounds, Ty reflected on the kid's account of what had happened the night Major Lange was murdered. He had to admit the kid's version fit together in a logical progression of events.

The deadly chain of actions and reactions was set in motion when the kid strong-armed Major Lange. This confrontation took place a few hours after he was soundly whipped in a croquet match. The kid freely admitted to robbing Lange, taking the $2 Ty had forced him to relinquish as compensation for breaking a mallet. Ty figured the kid could very well have spotted that coal prospector lounging in a miners' saloon just as he claimed he had. With a handlebar mustache, khaki duds, and lace-up boots, the gent stood out in cattle country.

In addition, Ty had no reason to doubt the kid's contention that he had purchased a jug of cheap wine. He probably guzzled it down just as he had guzzled whiskey in the bunkhouse, and perhaps he had passed out on the prairie just as he had stated. Awakening later, he headed for the Circle L on a slow horse. He had no other place to go.

Ty's gaze drifted down the plank walk toward Bertha's café. He saw Elizabeth Rogers coming. She carried a cloth-covered tray.

Ty caught himself staring. The style of her hair, swept to one side and pinned under a hat, reminded him a little of Sarah. With her back straight and shoulders squared, she walked in smooth strides, reminiscent of his wife's gait, too.

Elizabeth was older, of course. Watching her made him wonder how Sarah would have looked at a similar age, just as he sometimes wondered about the man his infant son would have grown into had he lived. Ty sometimes

155

dreamed about them. Moments ago a single mention of his wife and son in answer to the kid's halting questions had stirred memories.

Ty pushed dream images away, or tried to, as he moved to the door of the sheriff's office. He opened the door for Elizabeth, and gestured to the covered tray. "Beef stew and biscuits?"

"No, today we are serving biscuits and beef stew."

Ty grinned as he followed her into the sheriff's office.

Rogers was there, seated at his desk. He stood and came around it for the tray. Ty knew his policy called for an officer to deliver meals. Rogers took the tray from Elizabeth and carried it outside to the adjoining cell-block. Returning minutes later, he rejoined his wife and Ty in the office.

"Wade, wait till you hear what Ty just told me," she said.

The lawman's gaze swung from her to the ramrod. "Did the kid confess?"

Ty shook his head.

"You were in there with him for a long spell," Rogers said. "What did he tell you?"

"He figures he'll hang," Ty replied.

"So do I," Sheriff Rogers said.

"The kid said he wanted me to know the truth," Ty said. "Like you said, he figures he can trust me."

"But he didn't confess?" Rogers said.

"No," Ty replied. "He claims he's innocent."

Jaw clenched, the bearded lawman rejected that claim.

Elizabeth spoke up. "Wade, he says he knows who killed Major Lange."

"What's his story?" Rogers said.

"Tell him, Ty," she said.

Ty repeated the kid's accusation. He saw the sheriff

stiffen, reacting first with disbelief, then a visceral revulsion.

"The Durning sisters!" Rogers exclaimed. He shook his head in disgust. "He's just using you to shift the blame, Ty. He'll probably want you to testify in court for him. Don't worry. When I haul him before a judge, he won't get away with any shenanigans."

Elizabeth motioned to Ty to continue. "Tell him why he claims the sisters would do such a horrible thing."

Ty repeated the kid's account of events on the night of the murder.

Sheriff Rogers listened, glowering.

"He's right about one thing," the lawman said. "He can shout it to the heavens, but no one's going to believe that tale."

"Those two sisters couldn't have committed such a crime," Elizabeth said. Then she paused, clearly considering new information. Her gaze swung to her husband. "Could they?"

Sheriff Rogers shook his head. "No."

"Well . . . ," she began, and fell silent.

"Well, what?"

"Major Lange was small in stature," Elizabeth said after another moment of deliberation. "I suppose . . . well, I suppose his body would not be too heavy to move a short way. And that thermal spring isn't very far from the siding. . . ."

Rogers shook his head. "If you're building up a pile of horse manure the way I think you are, get that notion out of your head."

"Remember how those two sisters handled a croquet mallet," she said, adding: "You know what they say about a woman wronged."

Rogers continued glowering as he listened to his wife's speculations.

"I suppose they could have struck him on the head with a mallet," she said. "Couldn't they?"

Rogers spoke her name. "Elizabeth."

"I'm not saying they did," she said. "I'm just saying they could have." She added: "The two of them could have dragged his body to that thermal spring at night without being seen."

Her husband dismissed this line of reasoning with a single shake of his head. "No matter how you cut it, the kid's trying to shift the blame. He's trying to save himself. Most prisoners do. Sitting in a cell day and night, they don't have anything else to think about."

Elizabeth turned to Ty. "What do you think of the kid's story?"

"First time I heard it," he said, "I didn't believe it."

Sheriff Rogers looked at him in surprise.

Elizabeth said: "Sounds like you've changed your mind."

Ty did not reply until she pressed him.

"Have you?" she asked.

Ty answered by relating everything he knew and most of what he suspected. When he finished, Sheriff Rogers was not persuaded.

"If the kid claimed he was too drunk that night to know what he did or didn't do," the lawman said, "I'd be inclined to believe his yarn . . . or some of it. Maybe he did drink himself into a stupor. Maybe he doesn't remember what happened. That doesn't make him innocent."

Elizabeth said: "But, Wade. . . ."

He cut her off again. "There's plenty of evidence, and it all points to the kid."

"But what if . . . ?"

158

"What if I turn him loose," Rogers said, "so he can kill again."

"I'm not suggesting you should free him," she said.

"Good, because that kid's staying in jail until the circuit judge gets here," he said. "He can spin his yarn then."

Elizabeth asked: "When will the judge arrive?"

Sheriff Rogers picked up a telegrapher's half sheet of paper from his desk and scanned it. "According to the latest message off the wire, Judge Samuel R. Weston will be in Coalton in two weeks. He's set to come in on the four o'clock westbound."

"Wade, you should question Rose and Sharon beforehand," she said. "And Edgar and Millicent while you're at it. Question them separately so you can hear them out. Then you can compare their stories. . . ."

Rogers's beard seemed to bristle when he turned his full attention to her. "Elizabeth, this town is big enough for one sheriff."

"Oh, Wade, I'm not trying to tell how to run your office," she said, and proceeded to do just that. "That kid's life is at stake. The more I think about it, the more I think we might be overlooking some evidence. Something important." She moved a step closer to him and gestured to an adjoining room used by night deputies. "Question all four of them, and I'll transcribe your interviews in there. They can't see me. All you have to do is ask the right questions and compare their answers. . . ."

"I already spoke to the sisters," Rogers broke in. "I informed them they can expect to be questioned by the judge in a preliminary hearing. Sometime after that, they will be free to leave. It's all up to the judge."

"Wade, all that's routine procedure," Elizabeth said. "I mean you should question them in depth, separately.

Guilty or innocent, maybe you'll be the one to sort out the truth."

Ty saw husband and wife exchange hard stares in a protracted silence. Clearly a match for her man, Ty figured Elizabeth Rogers was not a woman to let go of a good idea without a struggle.

"How do you see this thing, Smitty?"

Ty posed that question after he crossed the street and met his top hand coming out of the Comet. The two men stood on the boardwalk by the tie rail where bands of autumn sunlight slanted across the graded street. After recounting his conversations with the kid and then with the sheriff and his wife, Ty waited for an answer.

Smitty cogitated, shifted his booted feet, and hemmed and hawed over the question of the night hawk's capacity for evil. For once the chief bunkhouse debater of the Circle L was momentarily silenced in the face of a dilemma.

"Reckon he aims to dodge the noose," Smitty said at last, "by blaming the sisters for the crime."

Ty said: "That's how Rogers sees it."

Smitty turned the tables on him. "How do you see this thing, Ty?"

"I know those two sisters were hopping mad at Major Lange for dragging them across the prairie like he did," Ty said. "He admitted he lied to them. The kid says he heard Lange break off his engagement to Rose. He said he was taking both ladies back to their mother." Ty thought it over. "I never figured the sisters could be mad enough to kill Lange. I thought the kid was wrong or lying about that. Maybe he is, and maybe he isn't. I remember you said you've ridden with some hardcases over the years. You said you didn't believe the kid was the killing kind."

160

"I remember muttering something like that," Smitty allowed.

Ty went on: "Sheriff Rogers said the same thing, more or less, when he first brought the kid to meet me here in town. Seems he changed his mind after that handbill came to the U.P. station."

"But what about the witness?" Smitty asked.

"Doesn't cut it with Rogers," Ty said. "He acts like the kid's been tried and convicted. As far as he's concerned, there's nothing left to do but knot the rope. I've been wondering if you've changed your mind, too."

"About the kid being a killer?" Smitty asked.

Ty nodded.

The ranch hand shook his head slowly. "Drunk or sober, I don't believe the night hawk would kill anyone . . . not out of revenge, anyway."

Ty shoved his hat up on his forehead as though shedding light on the subject. "The kid's hot-tempered half the time and wrong-headed most of the time. Taken altogether, though, I'm inclined to side with you."

Smitty asked: "Where does that leave us?"

"With chores hanging over our heads," Ty answered.

"Chores?"

"Elizabeth Rogers gave me an idea," Ty said. "I aim to have a talk with the sisters. I want to hear what they've got to say for themselves."

"I don't reckon I'll be much help to you, Ty. . . ."

Ty grinned at the tone of uncertainty in Smitty's voice. Clearly the ranch hand did not relish a confrontation with the Durning sisters.

"Fact is, Smitty, I'm a mite worried about the home place."

"Why's that?"

161

"I've been gone too long to know what's going on out there," Ty said. "If the spread is to be sold, the headquarters need to be in tip-top shape for the new owner. Circle L saddle mounts have to be tended and corralled, too. I'm putting those chores on your list."

Smitty nodded, obviously relieved to be assigned tasks he could readily handle. He glanced skyward. "I'll head for the Circle L as soon as I hit the saddle. I'll ride as far as I can before dark, and make a long ride to the home place tomorrow."

"Obliged," Ty said, adding: "Tell Corny I'm bringing a bonus for him. Alone out there all this time, he's earned it."

At the end of Front Street Ty crossed the tracks and made his way to the siding. He angled toward the four Pullman Palace cars, noting that the window shades were down.

Ty stepped up to the open vestibule between the parlor car and the sleeper. He rapped on the parlor car door. While he stood there, he noted the solid brass hardware—machined handles, hinges, and latches—fitted neatly into the doorjamb. The door itself was walnut with etched glass windows panes. The car was not merely luxurious in appointments, it was fashioned by craftsmen.

Ty saw shadows moving behind the windows. Hushed voices came from inside the car. When no one answered, he rapped on the door again, harder. Several more minutes passed before the door eased open a few inches.

"Yes?"

Rose pulled the door open. Ty saw Sharon hovering behind her. Beyond them stood a fainting couch and assorted upholstered chairs. To their right he saw the floor safe, vault door open, shelves empty.

Ty wondered what had happened to the money he had seen in there. He remembered seeing stacks of cash the evening Major Lange opened the vault to gain access to a humidor. Passing out cigars, he had invited his guests to an after-dinner smoke, brandy, and man talk.

"Ladies," Ty greeted the sisters now. He did not know what else to say. In that moment he was reminded of the uncomfortable silence during the evening meal served by Edgar and Millicent in the dining car.

"Is there something we can do for you, Mister Johnson?" Rose asked.

"I talked to the sheriff a while ago," Ty said. Hearing a tentative tone in his own voice, he cleared his throat and tried to come up with something besides spit. In truth Ty did not know what he should say to the sisters. He had no experience at questioning folks in the guise of idle conversation. Ladies in particular represented a challenge. Yet for his own satisfaction he knew he had to see this through.

"Precisely what were you talking about with the sheriff?" Sharon asked.

"We were going over things the night Major Lange was killed," he said, then added: "Precisely."

Rose stiffened as though detecting a note of sarcasm from an inferior. "I beg your pardon?" she said.

Ty was uncertain of her meaning, but went on, "What did you ladies see that night?" When neither one of them answered, he asked: "What did you hear?"

"I do not know what you are implying," Rose said, "but your questions are impertinent . . . impertinent and rude."

"To me as well," Sharon chimed in. "Impertinent. Rude. Yes."

"You told the sheriff," Ty said, "that you heard Major Lange arguing with my night hawk. Is that true?"

Rose stared at him. "Mister Johnson, everything we told the sheriff is true. I can assure you of that, just as I can assure you that I dislike your tone of voice and the implications of your words."

Behind her Sharon said: "Yes. Just what are you implying, Mister Johnson? That we lied?"

Ty was formulating an answer when Rose demanded: "Who sent you . . . that scruffy bumpkin who murdered the love of my life?"

"He says he heard the love of your life break off your engagement," Ty said. "Something was said about money. I'm wondering about that."

Rose demanded: "Wondering what?"

Ty pointed to the safe. "What happened to the money I saw in that vault?"

Rose gasped at his temerity even to raise the issue of theft. "Leave."

"Yes," Sharon said. "Leave us alone."

"My night hawk says you and Major Lange shouted up a storm," Ty said. "Caterwauling, he called it."

"A lie, of course," Rose said. "It is obvious. That boy will lie to save his skin."

Sharon's voice echoed behind her. "Yes. A bald lie."

"Reckon I'll have a talk with Edgar and Millicent," Ty said. "I figure they might have heard something that night. . . ."

Rose interrupted him. "I won't have you pestering the help, or anyone else. Have you no respect for our grief?"

Sharon said again: "Leave us alone, Mister Johnson."

"I'll leave," Ty said, "after I find out what happened to the money that was in that floor safe. . . ."

Tight-lipped, Rose glanced back at her sister. "Tell Edgar we need him."

Sharon turned swiftly and padded away, the fabric of her dress billowing behind her.

"I offer fair warning, Mister Johnson," Rose said. "Leave peaceably now. Or else."

"Or else what?" Ty asked.

She threw her head back. "You will find out to your great regret."

Ty said: "I don't savvy."

"You have undoubtedly noticed Edgar is a big, strong man," she said. "He can snap you like a twig. And he will do my bidding."

"I had a dog like that once," Ty said.

"You impudent boor," Rose said, her face flushed. "How dare you taunt me."

Ty met her unflinching gaze. He had been called names before, but never those two. He wondered about their meaning when heavy footfalls sounded. A looming shadow eased into his line of vision.

Edgar had appeared, behind Rose, like an oversize apparition. Sharon followed, hands pressed to her cheeks. Farther behind, Millicent came along, worry lines etched deeply in her face.

The manservant glowered at Ty. Fists clenched, he eased past the sisters.

"Miss Rose and Miss Sharon," he said to Ty, "asked you to leave."

"When I'm ready," Ty said, "I'll move along."

"You will move along now," Edgar said, adding: "Get out before I throw you out."

"Like you threw Major Lange's body into that hot spring?"

"What the hell?" he demanded. "What . . . what are you accusing me of?"

"I figure you know," Ty said, "if you hit Major Lange with a mallet and threw him into that spring. I'm asking you . . . man to man . . . did these two sisters pay you to take care of that chore, or did you do it on your own?"

Growling like an animal, Edgar advanced another step, fist up. "You've got a bad mouth, cowboy. Shut it while you still got some teeth."

"After you answer my question," Ty said, "you can crawl back under the rock where you came from."

The big man sneered. "You think you can whip me, cowboy?"

"Reckon that's a job for the equalizer," Ty said.

"Equalizer."

Ty drew his revolver. "Meet Mister Colt, the equalizer. The first bullet will punch a hole in the sky. The second one has your name on it."

The manservant warily eyed the handgun as Ty aimed it skyward. Cocking the hammer, he pulled the trigger. The revolver bucked in his hand. In the close quarters of the vestibule the report was deafening, loud enough to set ears ringing and nostrils stinging from acrid gunsmoke.

Rose and Sharon shrieked in terror. Mouths stretched open and eyes bulging, they backed away, clearly expecting this insane cowboy to kill them all. Edgar pulled back, too, pressing against them. His jaw had dropped open like a trap door, and now he staggered, a large man colliding with panic-stricken women.

"Reckon the next one has your name on it," Ty repeated to him. He squinted as he slanted the gun toward the light and made an elaborate pretense of examining the next bullet in the cylinder. "Sure enough," Ty said. "There it is. Plain as day . . . *Edgar.*"

Ty aimed the gun at him, cocking the hammer again.

The manservant spun away. He fled into the parlor car. In his haste to rush past Rose, he knocked her into Sharon, nearly toppling the sisters like bowling pins as he made good his escape. Lifting her dress, Millicent turned and hurried away.

Ty heard a distant shout. He saw Sheriff Rogers coming. Peacemaker in hand, the big lawman lumbered up the middle of Front Street toward the railroad tracks.

With their attention drawn by the gunshot, passers-by in town briefly halted. Gunfire was unusual in Coalton, but not without precedent. On occasion the gunsmith fired off a round or two to test a firearm, and at times celebrants cranked off a few rounds, day or night.

Now townsfolk peered in the direction of the Pullman cars. Sharing glances or a shrug, they looked at one another long enough to feel confident their sheriff had things under control, and continued on their separate ways.

Rogers stepped over the tracks. He shouted again, this time summoning Ty.

Easing the hammer down, Ty holstered his revolver. He stepped down from the vestibule to the railroad bed and waited there for the lawman. In the next moment he heard a sound behind him. He turned as Rose leaned into the vestibule from the safety of the parlor car.

"Sheriff!" she exclaimed. "Sheriff, arrest this man! Arrest him! He tried to kill us!"

Chapter Ten

"The sheriff arrested you, and then he let you go?" Smitty asked. "He should have hanged you while he had the chance."

Ty took a ribbing from Smitty. Next to him on the verandah, Corny cast a disapproving look at the ranch hand, as if hoo-rawing the ramrod amounted to disloyalty.

At the completion of his ride from town, Ty traded his saddle for the wicker armchair. Smoking his pipe, he buttoned his sheepskin against the chill in the air after sundown. Wearing jackets, too, Smitty and Corny sat on the edge of the verandah by the steps, one smoking, the other chewing.

Ty gazed at ranch buildings, fenced livestock, and the expanse of prairie beyond the home place. He had found everything to be in order upon his return—critters tended, eggs gathered, troughs filled, stalls mucked. After the brief inspection, he handed Corny a $10 gold eagle, a reward unexpected but not unearned.

"What happened, jailbird?" Smitty went on. "Did the sheriff toss you in the cell with your night hawk?"

Ty recounted details of his "arrest" by Sheriff Rogers in Coalton. In reality the lawman had held him in informal custody in the sheriff's office, until evening. Then he had fetched Ty's horse from the livery.

At nightfall the ramrod eased out of town without running afoul of the Durning sisters or anyone else objecting to a rancher firing his gun capriciously within town limits. Traveling by starlight, Ty camped beside a meandering creek several miles away from town. At first light he started out, heading for the home place.

Ty had spoken at length privately to Wade and Elizabeth Rogers before leaving Coalton. He recounted key events, mentioned the empty vault in the parlor car, and went on to describe his confrontation with the sisters and their manservant.

Ty reckoned he was a fair judge of horseflesh and men. While he did not pretend to divine a man's guilt or innocence by merely looking him in the eye, he suspected Edgar knew more than he had let on. When Ty had accused him of disposing of the body of Major Lange, Edgar's shifting gaze and wavering tone of voice signaled uncertainty. Taken altogether, Ty had reason to suspect the manservant was lying, or at least holding back.

Elizabeth listened intently to Ty. By now her line of reasoning to solve this crime approached the level of a personal crusade. This last observation from him only added weight and substance to her argument.

Ty noted Sheriff Rogers was uncharacteristically quiet, clearly chagrinned by her involvement in the investigation. From past conversations, Ty was aware the lawman had never before allowed his wife to be drawn into his work, not in his searches for fugitives, not in his investigations of local crimes. Much of what he encountered was tawdry, and he sheltered her from the worst of it. That was not difficult in years past because she had shown little interest in the details of his work. This case, though, had gotten under her skin. Like the rotten egg stench peculiar to the region, it would not go away.

Ty thought about that, searching for a reason for the inexplicable. Perhaps the sheer horror of it set this one apart from other crimes. The gruesome reality of a kindly man struck on the head with a croquet mallet and then dragged to the thermal spring where he had been shoved into boiling water constituted violent, vivid images.

An investigator into the cause of death could only wonder if Lange had been semi-conscious, dazed but still breathing when his killer rolled him into that hot pool. Had he regained consciousness the moment the scalding water had swept over him? No one would ever know, just as no one who saw it would forget the sight of a steaming corpse pulled out of the spring. Along with the fate of wandering drunks and misguided fools, folks whispered rumors of Major Lange cooked alive, screaming, just as the old tales claimed.

As horrible as it was, Ty figured Elizabeth would put the brutal crime to rest only after the murderer was brought to justice. For now, as to the crime, whether she would not let it go, or could not let it go scarcely mattered. After hearing Ty's account of his confrontation with the sisters, Elizabeth was further convinced.

"I think he's right, Wade," Elizabeth said in a low tone.

"Who?"

"That kid," she replied.

Ty stood by as a quiet tension mounted between them. He felt uncomfortable in his unintended rôle of eavesdropper, and fidgeted in the presence of husband and wife caught up in mid-argument.

He heard Elizabeth again insist her husband question

Edgar. He should query Rose, Sharon, and Millicent, too, and soon. She repeated her admonition to question the suspects separately. Now or never, she said, he must pry the truth out of them. The alternative was to allow a murderer to escape when the Pullman cars departed from Coalton, one bearing Major Lange's remains.

Ty glanced at Rogers, seeing three facets of one man. The long-suffering lawman stared into space; the husband hunkered down; the man waited for the storm to pass.

On the ranch Smitty asked Ty: "What about the night hawk?"

"He still figures he'll hang," Ty answered. "He doesn't expect to get a fair trial in Coalton."

"Will he?"

Ty shrugged. "My crystal ball is busted."

Corny spoke up. "I do believe he killed Lange."

Smitty cast a critical look at him.

"That kid cussed me every chance he got," Corny went on. "When he first came out here, I was gentle on him. I tried to set him straight. He took to cussing me." Corny paused. "He's got a mean streak running down his back, Ty. The night of the killing, he was drunk. When he's drunk, he goes from acting silly to being mad at the world. I do believe he went after Lange for his money."

"Plenty of folks in Coalton would agree with you," Ty conceded.

"The sheriff included?" Smitty asked.

Ty nodded. "But not the sheriff's wife."

Ty had never seen Arthur Blaine on horseback, and a week later when a lone rider wearing a full-length duster, riding boots, and a narrow-brimmed hat approached the home ranch, Ty did not recognize him until he heard a familiar voice.

"Good afternoon, Ty."

Ty squinted. "Blaine? That you?"

"It's me, all right," the banker replied. He gestured over his shoulder to indicate the breadth of Circle L range. "A long ride from town, isn't it? After all these years of living in Coalton, I never set foot on the Circle L until now."

Ty wondered what had brought him here.

Blaine drew rein. "Truth is I never got past the bottom line of your account in the bank, Ty."

Ty invited him to dismount. He knew better than to ask why Blaine was here. A banker never did anything without a reason, and he knew Blaine to be a straight-shooter. He figured he would find out soon enough.

Unexpected as this visit was, Ty figured Blaine's presence had some bearing on the arrival of the circuit judge in town. He guessed the judge had ordered depositions taken in the murder case lodged against the kid, and perhaps he had ordered Blaine to summon Ty for his testimony.

"After I tend that saddle mount from Jim's Livery," Ty said, "we'll see what Corny can scrape out of his cauldron. The cowhands tell me the saltiest chunks sink to the bottom. Might be a biscuit or two down there, too, heavy as stones."

"After two days on the trail," Blaine said, "hot food of any description suits me."

Ty observed the banker as he swung down. He took a few steps, stiff-legged from his ride. Ty took the reins and headed for the corral.

Looking around, Blaine nodded approvingly as he followed him. "A fine spread, the Circle L. Range laden with water and grass, prosperous as all hell with you running the operation."

"Much obliged," Ty said.

"Who's your hired man this year?"

"Smitty," Ty replied, adding: "I aimed for him and the kid to bust ice and buck snow through the winter."

"That was before the youngster got in trouble, eh?"

Ty nodded, and left it at that.

The banker halted at the pole corral. He braced a foot on the bottom rail and watched Ty turn the horse out in the corral. "You might be wondering what I'm doing out here, a humble townsman wandering so far from the comforts of home."

"Reckon I might be pondering just such a question," Ty allowed.

"You should be," Blaine said. "The answer concerns you."

"Me?" Ty said.

Blaine nodded.

"Should I be worried?"

"We'll both find out when we get to Coalton," he replied.

"Coalton," Ty repeated. "Hell, I just came from there."

"So did I," Blaine said. "We're going back."

Ty stared at him. "Not me."

"You may wish to reconsider," he said.

"Nope," Ty said, jaw clenched. "I've got work to do around here. This ranch doesn't run itself. You know that."

"I know Smitty and Corny can run things for a spell."

Ty shook his head. "What's this all about?"

"I don't know," Blaine replied, "but I know it's important. I wouldn't ask you otherwise."

Ty eyed him. He respected the banker and figured this

request was no wild-goose chase. But he had no wish to make another ride to Coalton, either. "Not now."

"Hear me out, Ty."

Jaw clenched, Ty nodded at him. "Let's get some chow."

Seated on benches at the long table in the mess hall, Ty listened to Arthur Blaine. In answer to his question, Ty learned the circuit judge had not yet arrived in Coalton.

As expected, the banker was not one to beat around the bush. Ty soon realized his ride to the ranch had a substantial reason behind it, one that had nothing to do with testimony in a hearing before the judge.

"The Lange estate," Blaine said, "is represented by the law firm of Reynolds and Ochs of Baltimore, Maryland. After learning of the untimely death of Major Lange, lawyers back there sent a flurry of messages to me by wire and by mail car. They are paying me one hundred dollars to deliver you to a sealed envelope in the bank."

Ty believed the banker had misspoken. "You mean to deliver an envelope to me?"

Blaine shook his head. "No, I do not mean that. My obligation is to escort you to the bank in Coalton. A sealed envelope bearing your name is locked in the vault. Until I complete the task of escorting you there, that is where the envelope will stay. It is to be opened by you, and only by you, with the county sheriff and me serving as witnesses. All parties must sign and swear to their signatures. If we cannot meet these conditions, the envelope is to be returned to Reynolds and Ochs, seal unbroken, contents intact. So the lawyers inform me."

Ty studied him, uncertain what it all meant and where this discussion was headed.

"I have a question to ask," Blaine said. "It's a bit embarrassing. Don't take it personally. In this case I am merely following orders."

Curiosity piqued, Ty asked: "What question?"

"I'll put it this way," he said. "If Tyler Johnson is not your real name, now is the time to tell me."

Ty met his gaze. He had never been involved in machinations like this, legal or otherwise, and he struggled to absorb the meaning of it. He figured the banker was instructed to ask that question as a means of determining guilt in crimes committed by Ty sometime in the past.

"Tyler Johnson is my right name."

"No middle name?" Blaine asked.

Ty shook his head. "My folks were frugal."

It was an old joke, one that drew a brief smile from the banker. "You'll swear to it?"

Ty nodded, his expression dead pan. "I'm frugal, too."

"So Tyler Johnson is your full name," Blaine said with finality. "That simplifies matters a bit."

Ty thought back over the maze of conditions and instructions he had just heard. "You're telling me we have to ride all the way to Coalton to get this thing done in your bank . . . whatever in the hell it is that we are getting done. Is that it?"

Blaine winced at the suggestion of a ride to town on horseback. "As saddle sore as I am now, Mister Tyler Johnson, that is exactly what I'm telling you. With the sheriff present, we will open said envelope in the privacy of the bank, after hours."

"What's in that envelope?" Ty asked.

"I do not know," Blaine said. "My understanding is no one outside the law firm of Reynolds and Ochs in Maryland knows, either."

* * * * *

Ty had learned from experience a sure-fire way to take the measure of a man was to herd cattle by day, chase runaway horses after nightfall, and share camp fare any time. On the trail the division of chores and coping with inevitable crises revealed more of a man's nature, as far as Ty was concerned, than any test that had ever been devised to plumb character and to gauge common sense.

Arthur Blaine, clearly out of his element crossing the prairie on horseback, grabbed the saddle horn with both hands and held on for dear life as he rode. His duds were soiled, much wrinkled by the conditions of a strenuous ride. Without complaint, though, he faced every obstacle they encountered on the trail and in camp. From swirling dust devils to an evening rain shower drowning their campfire, he retained his good humor even as the condition of his garb deteriorated.

They had not trailed cattle on this ride. With that exception to Ty's test, by the time they reached the livery in Coalton, he knew more than the scattered details of an upbringing Blaine had offered specifically or alluded to in general terms. Without knowing he was a subject undergoing the test, the banker proved his mettle just as Major Lange had proven his when he had ridden with Ty and Smitty to the coal seam and back.

Blaine had alerted Sheriff Rogers. He notified his deputies to hold their fire if they spotted three suspicious characters in the alley behind the bank. According to the plan, when the banker and the ramrod arrived in town on horseback, Rogers was to leave his office and angle across the street to the alley. They would all meet at the rear entrance to the bank.

Arriving on schedule, Rogers joined them. Blaine admitted them, and locked the door. He struck a match and fired a kerosene lamp. Dark shadows leaped away from the bright light when he held the lamp aloft. Blaine led the way through a short hallway to the room where the elaborately painted vault stood like a small-scale fortress.

Ty glanced around, feeling the tomb-like aura of this place. No one spoke. He figured they were silenced by the shadowed interior of an empty bank, a repository with dark spaces looming beyond the reach of the lamp.

Ty and the sheriff waited by a wooden railing separating teller cages from the desks of the bank president and head teller. Ty noted one maple desktop with an inkwell and pen. A green eyeshade had been left behind. He turned and saw the sheriff staring after the banker as he entered the back room.

Blaine set the lamp aside. He moved to the vault. Leaning close to the dials, he spun them clockwise, counter-clockwise, and clockwise again. Grasping the pair of handles, then, he turned them downward and took a step back to pull open the heavy doors. He reached in and re-trieved an outsize envelope.

Blaine backed away with the envelope under his arm. He closed the doors and spun the dials to calibrate new combinations to both locks. With a set of numbers known only to the banker, then, he turned and came to the railing. He thrust the envelope out to Ty.

"This is what I meant," Blaine said to him, "when I told you I had been instructed to deliver you to an envelope."

Ty took it from his outstretched hand. For a long moment he gazed at his name, *Tyler Johnson*, the letters penned in a sweep of curving script on the face of the envelope. A simple name, he thought, one never before inscribed in such elaborate cursive.

Mister Tyler Johnson
C/O Circle L Ranch
Coalton, Colorado

Ty looked to the banker for guidance. Blaine picked up the lamp and nodded once as he motioned to the envelope. His message was unspoken, yet clear: *This is the appointed hour.*

Ty broke the seal.

Opening the flap, he pulled out a folded map. He opened it, studied it for a moment, and turned it right side up. Paper rattled as he slanted it toward the lamplight. The Official State of Colorado map defined the boundaries of the Circle L Ranch. Property lines were diagramed, initialed by surveyors, and updated on a map of the county. Boundaries included the recent purchase of homestead sections in the north sector, range land that had reverted to the state until purchased by Major Gregory Lange.

By lamplight Ty examined other papers. Most were property deeds to parcels noted on the county map, joined together with water and mineral rights intact. All were legally claimed and owned by Major Gregory Lange.

Ty discovered another, smaller envelope, and pulled it out of the large envelope. He opened the flap. A single sheet of paper, folded into thirds, was inside. He pulled it out and unfolded it. Held toward the light, Ty was shocked by the words printed across the top: **Last Will & Testament**.

"Read it aloud, Ty," Blaine said.

He did so, his voice quavering and tongue stumbling over nearly every word: " 'Of alert mind and sound body on this date, by my own free will, in the event of my death I hereby bequeath and award title and full ownership of the

Circle L Ranch, as defined herein, to my loyal employee of these many years, Mister Tyler Johnson. Upon my death, the Circle L Ranch in its entirety will transfer immediately and without encumbrances to Mister Tyler Johnson. This stipulation includes all bank accounts bearing my name in the First National Bank of Coalton, Colorado.' "

Ty stared at the signatures of two witnesses. Both were bank employees. He understood the words of the document he had just read, yet at once he felt baffled by the contents. The silence was broken when Arthur Blaine spoke to him.

"Congratulations, Mister Tyler Johnson."

Ty turned to him, wondering at the banker's formality.

"You are now sole owner of one of the finest ranches in Colorado," Blaine said.

Ty shook his head slowly. The enormity of it swept over him like a wave from a cold sea. *You are now sole owner. . . .*

This was a time for solemn handshakes and muted celebration. Muted, for the three of them knew, of course, that a man had to die for his last wishes to be enacted by the provisions of his will. Thus, sorrow combined with joy in a strange alchemy of contrasting emotions.

They did not tarry. With the Circle L documents locked in the vault where rushing waters were depicted in a mountain scene, the three men parted in the pitch-black darkness of the alley behind the bank. The banker and the lawman wished Ty well in his endeavors on the ranch. Blaine spoke of home and a worried wife waiting up for him, a wife who knew all to well he was no horseman. Blaine bid the sheriff and the rancher good night.

As a favor to him, Ty led the rented saddle mount as well as his own horse to Jim's Livery. He was accompanied by Sheriff Rogers as far as the corral. There, with a last congratulatory slap on the back, the lawman headed for home.

In the livery Ty went through the motions, chores second nature to him since his youth working as a wrangler and night hawk on the Bar 10. With no need to roust the liveryman so late at night in his residence, Ty stripped both horses, combed them, and grained them. All the while he felt dazed by what had just happened, as though mind and body had somehow cleaved.

Leaving the livery, he headed for the Comet. By the glow of street lamps, this end of town was familiar terrain—or should have been familiar to him. It was, and it wasn't. In truth, he was a man traipsing through a dreamscape on Front Street.

He followed the plank walk crowded with passers-by coming and going from the saloon district. Townsmen and women did not yet know of his inheritance, a fact further deepening the mental schism, the detached sensation of his state of mind. He had not felt a disorientation of such magnitude since the kid had sucker-punched him.

Reaching the Comet now, Ty shoved batwing doors apart and entered. He crossed the room, feeling warmth emanating from a coal-fueled heater. At the bar, Ty signaled Ray. He turned, then, noting the image of a grizzled ranch hand reflected in the outsize mirror.

That can't be me, he thought.

Ray welcomed him. " 'Evenin', Ty."

"Howdy," Ty replied.

Turning away from the mirror, Ty's gaze swept past the barman. He took in the saw-dusted floor, mounted heads of animals, and pressed tin ceiling. In his disembodied state, he might have been seeing the decor for the first time.

Ray brought a mug of beer topped by a two-inch head. He slid it across the bar.

"How are you?" Ray asked him.

180

Ty shoved his sweat-rimmed hat up on his forehead. That query was often posed among friends and strangers, yet rarely was it answered with candor. Instead of a perfunctory reply, Ty gave serious thought to it as he pulled a nickel out of his pocket.

"Never better," he said, sliding the coin toward him.

"Glad to hear it," Ray said with a grin. Pocketing the coin, he moved down the length of the bar.

Ty's thoughts drifted to Major Lange. He lifted his mug in a silent tribute. Memories wandered. His acquaintanceship with Lange, certainly the most unusual of his life, was one he would never forget, inheritance notwithstanding.

Ty wondered when the man had bumped up against his mortality. What were the circumstances that drove him to pen his will? Was the decision in some way fueled by the death of Bill Connors? The row with his fiancée? Had Lange feared for his life?

Ty did not know the answers, and supposed he might never know. He did know, however, his inheritance would be common knowledge in Coalton all too soon, and at some point word of it would carry throughout the county and even the state. He knew, too, the transition from ranch manager to stockman was far beyond the scope of his experience.

Ty thought about that. He figured most men nurtured dreams of acquiring wealth, somehow, some way, whether it was out of the blue, a turn of the card, or a roll of the dice. Such dreams were rarely stated aloud, if ever. A fantasy given voice only led to dissatisfaction with one's lot in life.

Ty wondered how folks would react when they learned of his windfall. Good wishes? Jealousy? Envy? Indifference?

Now that he thought of it, he wondered how the

Durning sisters would react. The kid said the dispute he had overheard the night of the murder indicated money had been an issue, perhaps the lynch pin of the relationship between Major Lange and Rose.

If Ty slept at all that night, he had little memory of it later. What would stick in his memory was lying awake in a lumpy, smelly rooming house bed with a stinking pillow. The 30¢ rented room was near the railroad tracks. Raucous sounds from the saloon district reached him like murmurs of distant voices, sounds punctuated by the shouts of men and the squeals of women.

Frugal, it had not occurred to him that he could have spent the night in the Coalton House. A hot bath would have been welcomed, as would supper and breakfast in the hotel restaurant. His wealth would have covered such expenses easily. . . .

When at last he drifted off to sleep, he overslept until a train whistle sounded. Startled by the blasts, Ty left the bed. He checked his pocket watch in his trousers. Time that had seemed like minutes was in fact several hours in duration. He turned to the window and raised the shade, greeted by a surprise outside.

Quiet as a cougar, a cloud bank had settled over Coalton last night. Five or six inches of snow had drifted out of a cold sky, blanketing the ground. A packed cushion of snow on Front muffled the iron-tired wagon wheels of passing coaches and freight outfits. Ty figured softened sounds from the street had finally lulled him to sleep before dawn, a deep sleep until the train whistle speared the quietude.

Ty dressed and pulled on his boots. He put on his sheepskin and grabbed his hat as he left the rooming house. Outside, dry snow creaked under his boots as he gingerly strode down the block toward Bertha's Home Cooking Café. At once he knew word was out, that rumors had spread through Coalton like a wind-driven fire.

Ty knew this by the reaction of townsmen and women who observed him. Over the years many of them had come to know him by sight if not by name. Now they cast lingering looks at him from either side of the snow-covered street. Some stopped and stared. From others, snatches of hushed conversations drifted to him.

"That's him. . . ."

"Him?"

"Yeah, that rancher. . . ."

"Name's Johnson. . . ."

"They call him Ty. . . ."

"Inherited a fortune. . . ."

When he knocked snow off his boots upon entering the café, he was boldly greeted by Bertha herself. "Tyler! Tyler, is it true? Is it?"

"Is what true?" he asked, seeing a woman who seemed ready to explode.

"You know what," she said.

"Tell me what I know," he replied with a quick grin.

Exasperated, she demanded: "Did you inherit the Circle L like folks are claiming?"

"Bertha. . . ."

Without waiting for his answer, she charged onward. "The whole kit and caboodle? Did you? All morning folks are saying you did. They're saying that rich man from Maryland, that Major Lange gent who got killed, he named you in his will. Did he? Well, did he?"

"Reckon he did," Ty replied.

"No!" she exclaimed.

Ty nodded.

"No!"

He nodded again.

"Oh, Tyler!"

Her excitement had not abated when he sat by the window that looked out on a world turned white. He looked out to Front while she carried on. Each windowpane framed a street scene in lace-like frost. Bertha brought a bowl of beef stew and two buttered biscuits to him, whether he wanted them or not, and resumed exclaiming over his good fortune.

"Oh, Tyler, I can't believe it! I just can't! The whole kit and caboodle!"

"I've had some trouble swallowing it myself," he allowed as he eyed the stew.

Bertha laughed in hearty glee. "Oh, Tyler! The Circle L! The whole ranch! It's yours! Ain't that something? Ain't it, though?"

Pressing business, namely serving paying customers who had disembarked from the train, took her away from Ty's table. In the next moment his attention was drawn from the café's interior to the window. Framed in white frost, he glimpsed a gent passing by on the boardwalk. The man wore a canvas coat, straw hat, and sported a handlebar mustache.

Ty shoved his chair back. He got his feet under him and rushed to the door. Bertha hollered at him as he left steaming stew, his sheepskin coat and stockman's hat behind. He yanked open the door and ran outside. He turned sharply—or tried to.

Like a hog on ice, his feet went out from under him. He came to earth, hard. Landing on his right hip and shoulder, he rolled onto his back. He lay sprawled halfway on the snow-covered walk and halfway in the street under a tie rail.

He heard a feminine voice. A woman standing over him

184

asked if he was hurt. She called him by name, her tone of voice concerned. The voice was familiar, but he needed a moment to identify Elizabeth Rogers framed against clouds in the sky. She wore a hooded cloak and held an empty tray in her mittened hands. Ty figured she had come to the café to pick up a meal for the prisoner. Now she knelt at his side.

"Ty, are you all right?" she asked again.

Ty drew a deep breath. He exhaled a cloud as he looked skyward. He got his wits about him, sat up, and took inventory. "My pride's hurt purty bad," he answered.

"You aren't dressed for winter," she observed, and straightened.

Ty raised up to his knees and got to his feet. Passers-by resumed passing by. Brushing snow off his clothes, he looked down the way. A block and a half away he spotted the distinctive straw hat on the head of the man he sought.

"I have to get a rope on that gent," he said.

"Who is he?" Elizabeth asked, following his gaze.

"Coal prospector," Ty said.

"Why do you need to see him?" she asked.

"The kid talked about him," Ty said. "Claimed he followed him out of town the night Major Lange was killed."

Elizabeth stared as she grasped the significance of this assertion.

Chapter Eleven

Ty strode gingerly along the boardwalk, then jogged through loose snow in the street as he closed the distance. He caught up with the gent in the next block.

"Hold on!" Ty called.

The gent glanced over his shoulder, but did not slacken his pace.

"Hold on," Ty repeated. "We have a thing or two to talk over."

The gent halted. He turned to face him, clearly annoyed at being accosted by a stranger. "What do you want?"

"You don't remember me, do you?" Ty asked. He eyed the waxed mustache and the clean shave of his jaw.

"Can't say I do," the gent said. He cast a critical eye at Ty, from bare head to boot toes, clearly wondering why this man was not dressed for cold weather.

"A while back you crossed Circle L range," Ty reminded him, "after you grained your horse and pack mule. You took a meal in my mess hall, and rode out."

"Circle L," he repeated. "You the ramrod out there?"

"That's right."

"Yeah, I recollect now," he said. He paused. "I'll ask you one more time. What the hell do you want?"

186

"Coal prospector, aren't you?"

"What if I am?"

"I found your diggings," Ty said, adding: "On my land."

The gent stared at him, unmoving, as though he figured he could stonewall his way out of this confrontation.

Ty pressed him. "You didn't tell me you were prospecting when you crossed my land."

"Wasn't any of your damned business," he said.

"Trespassing on Circle L range is my business," Ty countered. "So is staking out the coal deposit."

"That's not your property up there," he insisted. "I know. I've seen the maps."

"You'd better look at those county maps again," Ty said.

"Why should I?"

"I have the deeds to prove ownership," Ty said.

The prospector glowered.

"The coal seam you were digging into is the north sector of the Circle L," Ty went on. "Go ask the land agent again. Tell him I sent you. Maybe you'll get the right answer this time."

The challenge drew a hostile look. "What if I don't believe a word you're saying, mister?"

"Then we'll take it up with the county sheriff," Ty said.

The two men regarded one another, each one clearly weighing the odds of coming out on top in a fight. The prospector's canvas coat was buttoned against the cold, denying him ready access to the sidearm that made a bulge at his waist. Ty's revolver, holstered, was within reach.

To underscore this advantage, Ty's right hand drifted toward the walnut grips of his Colt. He saw a look of uncertainty creep into the prospector's face.

Ty did not let on, but he was not eager to press this man any further. Having witnessed fights over the years and

187

having taken part in his fair share, he wanted a peaceful settlement. Once fists were flying and guns were drawn, deadly consequences could spin out of control.

Ty let him off the hook. "If you can answer a question for me, we'll straighten this thing out without butting heads."

The prospector's eyes narrowed. "What question?"

"A man got killed here in Coalton," Ty said. "His body was shoved into a hot spring outside of town."

"I heard about that," the prospector said, jaw clenched. "If you think I had anything to do with it, you're wrong. I was headed for that coal seam, miles away from Coalton when it happened."

"I don't think you had anything to do with the killing," Ty said. "I want to know if anyone saw you out there."

"No," he said, and then reconsidered. "Some kid."

"What kid?"

"A drunk kid riding a sway-backed horse out there on the prairie," he answered. "I heard him singing and shouting until he passed out."

"How do you know he passed out?" Ty asked.

"I doubled back when he quit his damned hollering," he replied. "Found him with an empty jug cradled in his arms, snoring up a storm. I left him there, and headed for the coal seam."

"That's the answer to my question," Ty said.

"What of it?" he asked.

"Tell it to the sheriff," Ty said, "and I won't lodge a charge of trespassing against you."

"Tell what to the sheriff?" he asked.

"What you just told me," Ty said. "Tell him the unvarnished truth. Then go take another look at those maps in the land agent's office. Like I said . . . the coal deposit, the marsh, and the surrounding terrain all the way to the Wyoming line is Circle L range."

"Told you," the kid said when he stepped out of the cellblock.

Ty stood by, watching him as he looked around at the snow-covered earth, eyes blinking against the white glare. Instead of shouted recriminations and bloody threats, the kid simply informed Sheriff Rogers of his innocence.

"Told you I never killed nobody."

Rogers had interviewed the coal prospector to his satisfaction, and now he conceded that point but offered no apology for jailing him. "You're free to go."

The kid's gaze swung from Sheriff Rogers to Ty. "Reckon I'll stick with the Circle L if the foreman still has a bunk for me."

"That's the owner you're talking to," Elizabeth Rogers said with a smile.

Before the kid could question her about that, Ty said: "Reckon I can locate an extra sougan or two, son."

From the sheriff's office Ty took the kid to Bertha's café. She cast a look of distrust at him before turning her attention to Ty. She demanded explanations. Why had he rushed out of the café? Why had he left his coat and hat and a bowl of stew behind? Did he aim to pay for cold food? Of course he would, Bertha said in answer to her own question. He was a rich rancher now.

"Ain't that right, Ty?" she asked. "You're a rich rancher since you inherited the Circle L."

Before Ty could reply, Bertha drew a deep breath and again trumpeted his good fortune. This reference was the first the kid had heard about that provision in Major

Lange's will. When Bertha ran out of wind, she headed for the kitchen.

The night hawk gawked at Ty across the table. "The Circle L . . . it's your ranch now . . . cattle, horses, buildings, everything?"

Ty nodded. "Reckon so."

"How'd that happen?"

"I've been wondering the same thing," Ty said, "ever since I read Major Lange's will."

The comment was lost on the kid. "What do you mean?"

"If I hadn't seen the will and property deeds myself," he replied, "I would never have believed the estate of Major Lange named me to inherit his ranch."

Still staring, the kid let this information sink in. "You'll hire a full crew next spring, won't you?"

Ty nodded. "Full crew come spring. Business as usual."

The kid looked at the frosted windowpane. "With all of that snow out there, spring seems like a long way off."

"It'll get here soon enough," Ty said. "Then we'll complain about the mud."

The kid thought about that. "If you and Smitty help me break that broomtail mare you gave me, she'll be ready for working cattle in spring roundup."

Ty considered the implications of this notion. The kid was still determined to ride for the Circle L.

"Reckon so, son."

A stranger arrived in Coalton on the train that day. Even without a stovepipe hat, at six feet he cut a Lincolnesque figure with a scrawny neck, prominent Adam's apple, and platter-size ears. Dressed in black from bowler to boots, his appearance that was reminiscent of old Abe was further emphasized by the swallowtail coat he wore.

This lanky gentleman strode purposefully along the snow-covered plank walk. Folks in his path parted, stepping aside to avoid impeding what must have been important business even though no one knew what it was. He carried a silver-headed walking stick, and used it to some advantage as he made his way on packed snow from the depot to the Coalton House, and finally to the sheriff's office. There, he announced his presence in a booming voice.

"Good day!" he said to all who had gathered in the office. "I am Samuel Weston, Judge Samuel Weston." He turned to Rogers. "You, sir, must be Sheriff Wade Rogers."

It was a safe bet, with Rogers being the only one wearing a badge.

The lawman stood. He reached across his desk, grasping Weston's hand in a vigorous shake. He introduced his wife. Ty came next. Last was the kid identified simply as "the night hawk".

The judge shook hands with all of them. "Gentlemen and lady," he said, "I have received brief messages by telegraph from the Coalton station, nothing more. I understand you are in need of a judge to initiate legal proceedings, namely a preliminary hearing in the crime of murder. Is that correct?"

"Yes, sir," Rogers replied.

"Then I must ask," he said with a broad smile of anticipation, "where do we begin?"

Sheriff Rogers's plan quickly took shape, previously discussed and now modified by suggestions from Elizabeth. Separate the sisters, she believed, and one might break. She also sensed Millicent was vulnerable and should be questioned aggressively. After some more discussion, a plan of action was confirmed by the sheriff and seconded by the judge.

With their strategy agreed upon, the five of them left the sheriff's office and swiftly made their way through the snow to the Pullman cars on the siding.

The judge led the way. He mounted the steps to the vestibule and knocked on the door to his left. When no answer came, he turned and rapped firmly on the other door. Presently it opened. Met by Rose and Sharon, the judge introduced himself.

The two sisters were deferential at first. But when they understood Judge Weston meant to search all four cars from top to bottom and side to side, Rose simply pointed to the door and ordered him out. Expecting to be obeyed, she reacted angrily when she discovered his authority as an officer of the court extended to her. He would not be dissuaded, and she would have to do as she was told. Forced to sit in their parlor car and wait, both sisters howled as though stung. Threats followed protests, all of them ignored by the judge.

With his muscular arms folded across his chest, Edgar offered no resistance. Millicent stood at his side and quietly wept, her chin quivering.

While searches were undertaken by Judge Weston, Sheriff Rogers, Elizabeth, Ty, and the kid, the sisters were flushed with anger, their voices choked by frustration. The kid threw clothing aside in a mad search for money. His rude actions stirred their wrath as no other.

"You do not have permission to violate our privacy!" Rose said at last. "In particular, I will not allow this foul youngster to paw through my clothing or touch my garments with his filthy hands."

"You may wait here quietly, Miss Durning," Judge Weston explained to her, "or you may wait in a cell while this unpleasant task is completed. What is your wish?"

Red-faced and jaws set, neither Rose nor Sharon offered an answer. The reason for their howls and threats of retribution was soon apparent. It did not take long for the searchers to find cash in hatboxes and steamer trunks, as well as more currency jammed into high-button shoes. In contrast, not a dime was found in the sleeper car or the parlor car used by Major Lange.

Ty saw Elizabeth take Millicent's arm and ease her aside. He overheard her inform the woman that her testimony would be sworn on a Bible.

"Do you know you will be arrested and jailed as an accomplice if you lie to the judge?" Elizabeth asked.

Shaken, eyes downcast, Millicent shook her head. "It is not my place. . . ."

"Your place is to be truthful," Elizabeth said softly.

Millicent turned to Edgar for guidance. He nodded once.

"I will never lie," Millicent whispered, and repeated her words to Judge Weston.

All of them watched as she turned to Rose and lifted her hand, pointing at her. "She . . . she and Sharon . . . they did it."

"Miss Sharon Durning and Miss Rose Durning killed Major Gregory Lange?" the judge demanded.

Millicent nodded. "Yes, sir."

"Told you," the kid said to anyone who would listen.

His words lit a short fuse. Both sisters shouted their defiance. Both claimed innocence. Millicent confessed knowledge of the crime, not guilt, a distinction confirmed by Edgar. Rather than go to a cell himself, he implicated the two sisters in the slaying of Major Lange. He had seen Rose take up a croquet mallet and he had overheard the fight between her and Major Lange. By starlight he had seen the two women dragging the body away from the Pullman cars toward the thermal spring.

Sharon denied guilt again, and tried to blame the kid. Her accusations fell apart when Rose acknowledged her rôle in a dispute with Major Lange, a fight that she admitted had escalated to violence. One truthful word broke ground for another, and presently the whole truth came out in a burst of rage.

"He lied," Rose explained, and repeated her condemnation of Major Gregory Lange. "He lied to me and he lied to Sharon."

"Lied about what?" Judge Weston asked.

"We were engaged to be married," she answered. "He promised a life of comfort for both my sister and me. It was a sacred promise. He lied about it just as he lied about our trek to that miserable ranch. He lied again and again to us."

Under pressure generated by the booming voice of Judge Weston, Rose admitted clubbing Lange at the height of fury in their last argument. She felt justified. The fault lay with him, she insisted, and he paid a dear price for his deceptions. In the end the sisters had no choice but to drag his body to the thermal spring and roll it into boiling water there. The spring reeked of sulphur, Rose said, a rotten odor associated with the gates to hell.

Ty saw the night hawk flinch when Rose raised her voice in a tone shrill enough to set things right once and for all. "Major Lange went to hell! He will spend eternity with the damned. That's where the liar belongs. Boiling in the stench of hell. For eternity!"

In the warming spring season Ty and Smitty covered the north sector of the ranch. They rode in wide circle around the coal seam and the tumble-down homesteader's cabin.

The log structure was leaning but still standing, just as they had left it last fall when the kid was taken away in irons by Sheriff Rogers.

Now, with no recent tracks left by shod hoofs in the soft earth, Ty was satisfied the coal prospector was long gone. He and Smitty made camp that evening. They pulled up the prospector's stakes and fed them to their campfire.

"Smitty," Ty said, waving smoke away from his eyes, "if you had some notion of carving a ranch out of this sector, where would you start?"

"With the marsh," Smitty said immediately. "That's your water supply. A cattle ranch should be mapped out from there to take in all of these acres of grassland."

Ty saw Smitty lift his arm in a sweeping gesture to include miles of prairie in every direction. "That's how I see it, too."

Smitty eyed him. "You're not thinking about selling off a piece of the Circle L, are you, Ty?"

Ty shook his head. "I'm thinking about giving away a piece."

"Giving?" Smitty repeated.

"Yeah," Ty said.

"Who to?" the ranch hand asked.

"You," Ty replied.

Shocked, Smitty stared at him across the flames of the fire.

"If you'd be interested," Ty added.

"Hell, yes, I'd be interested," the ranch hand said. "Who wouldn't be?" He struggled to find the right words, and came up with one: "Why?"

"I've been thinking things over all winter," Ty answered. "Major Lange was generous, the most generous man I ever met. In my own way, I aim to follow his track. But why wait until you read my will? I don't need this land to make a living from a cattle and horse operation." He added: "Besides, with you ranching in these parts, I can be sure of two things."

"What are they?" Smitty asked.

"Losing my top hand," he replied, "and gaining a good neighbor."

Smitty smiled and shook his head in disbelief. "Ty, I wasn't expecting anything like this. You sure you want to give away such fine range land? Land with water and a coal deposit?"

"I'm sure," Ty said. "We'll work out the boundaries with the land agent next time we go to Coalton."

On the ride back to Circle L headquarters Ty reflected on the recent past. He knew time brought changes, and he knew changes were rarely predictable. On the home place the kid was no longer belligerent. More surprising, he had made peace with Corny and now worked at his chores without complaint. Even Corny was impressed by the night hawk's change of mood.

Ty was surprised by an unexpected visit from Sheriff Rogers. The kid emerged from the cook shack and led the lawman's horse into the corral. Ty feared the worst. He suspected the lawman had come to arrest the kid. He could think of no other reason for him to make the two-day ride out here.

Instead, Rogers brought good news. The youngster who had murdered a girl in Denver was apprehended by federal marshals. He had been positively identified by the female witness, and jailed.

"I rode out here to tell you I'm sorry," Rogers said to the kid.

"Sorry?" the kid mumbled.

196

Ty could see the night hawk was mystified—and mistrustful. He figured the kid had never received an apology before.

"I'm sorry about the way I treated you," Rogers went on. "I figured you were guilty. A lot of folks did, but that's no excuse. I was wrong. Dead wrong. I should have listened to Elizabeth and questioned the sisters and the servants sooner, instead of waiting for the judge to get there."

Ty saw Rogers extend his hand. The kid shook it. Ty kept his thoughts to himself. He figured Elizabeth's advice had prompted this gesture of apology, and now it was done.

Sheriff Rogers ate in the mess hall that evening and slept in the bunkhouse that night. He had brought a stack of back issues of the *Rocky Mountain News* and *The Police Gazette* for the hands to read at their leisure. After breakfast at dawn, the kid brought the sheriff's horse around. He held it while the big man mounted. From the saddle Rogers's lifted his hand to his hat brim and bid them good bye.

In the evening Ty heard a knock on the ranch house door. He put down the *Rocky Mountain News* he was reading and opened the door. The kid stood on the porch. He thrust an issue of the *Gazette* into Ty's hands.

"Read this," he said.

"What is it?" Ty asked.

Holding the paper toward the lamplight, the kid traced his finger along a news account published in bold type.

The sport of croquet has been banned in Boston, Massachusetts. Good riddance to mallets of forethought. When will other cities take up the banner? In this so-called "sport" the male antagonist becomes a creature too vile for language. Worse, in every match the fine and

lovely decency of womanhood has disappeared by the third wicket.

"Told you," the kid said, and abruptly left the porch with the publication folded under his arm.

Grinning, Ty closed the door. His gaze swung to the framed photographic portrait propped up on his roll-top desk. The faces of his wife and son peered out at him, their expressions captured in a photographer's studio long ago.

Ty would never know the direction of his life if Sarah and Will had survived the flu epidemic. He would never know how his son would have turned out. In a strange way the night hawk left him with such wondering.

About the Author

Stephen Overholser was born in Bend, Oregon, the son of Western author, Wayne D. Overholser. He grew up in Boulder, Colorado where he lives with his family. Convinced, in his words, that "there was more to learn outside of school than inside," he left college in his senior year. He was drafted and served in the U. S. Army in Vietnam. Completing his military service, he launched his career as a writer while working the swing shift as a laborer in a sawmill and later as night custodian in elementary schools. He wrote fiction in his spare time, publishing short stories in *Zane Grey Western Magazine* and *Mike Shayne Mystery Magazine*, and *Anteus*, a literary journal. School vacations and weekends provided opportunities for research trips to libraries and archives throughout the intermountain West. On a research visit to the Coe Library on the Laramie campus of the University of Wyoming, he came across an account of a shocking event preceding the Johnson County War in Wyoming in 1892. The cattle war became the background for his first novel, *A Hanging in Sweetwater* (1974), awarded the Spur by the Western Writers of America. *Molly and the Confidence Man* (1975) followed, the first in a series of books about Molly Owens, a clever, resourceful, and tough undercover operative working for a fictional detective agency in the Old West. Among the most notable of Stephen Overholser's later titles are *Search for the Fox* (1976), *Track of the Killer* (1982), *Dark Embers at Dawn* (Five Star Westerns, 1998), *Cold Wind* (Five Star Westerns, 1999), *Shadow Valley Rising* (Five Star Westerns, 2002) and *Chasing Destiny* (Five Star Westerns, 2005). Stephen Overholser's next **Five Star Western** will be *Luke Siringo, United States Marshal.*